Perfectly Ernest

E.J. Wesley

To Jeannie,

Thank you for reading!

[signature]

Also by E.J. Wesley

The Moonsongs Series

(New Adult/urban fantasy/novella/serial)

http://www.ejwesley.com/moonsongs-series.html

SEASON ONE

Blood Fugue, Moonsongs Episode 1

Witch's Nocturne, Moonsongs Episode 2

Dark Prelude, Moonsongs Episode 3

SEASON TWO

Dragon's Game, Moonsongs Episode 4

Vampire's Ball, Moonsongs Episode 5

Devil's Snare, Moonsongs Episode 6

Get all of my latest news delivered right to your inbox! http://www.ejwesley.com/newsletter.html

Contents

Dedication

This one is for my family. Trees are only as strong as their roots, and people as sturdy as the foundations of love they stand upon. If there is strength in me, it comes from you.

Author's Note

Thank you for choosing to read Perfectly Ernest! As in real life, many of the characters in this story are struggling with mental illness. Unlike real life, their struggle is over in only a few hundred pages.

While my educational background is in counseling, and I spent a few years working in the field in various capacities, this is a work of fiction. I do not, nor could I ever, truly capture the depths of what it means to live with mental illness (or live with and love those who do). Consequently, my primary directive was to tell Ernie's story, entertain, and perhaps enlighten. But not to educate.

For that, there are far better resources than my overactive imagination. One such institution is the National Alliance On Mental Illness (NAMI www.nami.org). I will be donating 10% of the annual proceeds of Perfectly Ernest to them. If you or someone you know is suffering from mental illness, or you are simply curious to learn more, I encourage you to check them out.

Open discussion, education, and getting help are the keys to combatting these diseases. We can all make a difference.

Thanks for contributing to the cause. I hope you enjoy the read!

E.J. Wesley

Chapter One

I stepped off the pitching rubber and ground my cleats into the dirt mound like it was the face of my worst enemy. But, all I needed was a good mirror to find the real bad guy.

The tangy smell of fresh-cut grass mingled with the rich odors of hot, buttered popcorn and moist, tilled earth drifted on a subtle breeze. Sunlight, just strong enough to warm my face but not make me sweat, filtered down between a few lonely clouds. The first insects of spring buzzed around my ears. Although I'd blocked most of the distractions to a distant part of my mind, the chant of my name coming from the crowd in increasingly insistent, pulsing waves of sound created a different kind of buzzing in my stomach.

My closest friends—both eager and nervous—cheered for me, and I recalled a line from a Robert Frost poem I'd read before the game:

1

Not far, but near, I stood and saw it all.

This was a perfect moment, on a perfect day. Yet, I knew the dark cloud that had followed me most of my life was still there, waiting to unleash one hell of a storm.

I slapped my mitt against my thigh. *Fuck me.*

My concentration slipped. The excited hum of the stadium turned into a calamity of voices.

"Time!" The umpire's bellow cut through the racket.

I crammed the baseball back into my mitt, glared at the sky, and waited for the pointless intervention. My mind was made up. This would be my moment of inglorious failure, my final act of defiance. I felt relieved.

Junkyard would be the first one out to see what the hell was going on inside my head. Every good catcher was Freud to his pitcher's crazy, and Junk was a damn good catcher.

When I finally lowered my gaze, Junk trotted toward me in that awkward badger-like gait only catchers could master. Oddly enough, Junkyard kind of looked like a badger, too. He had compact, bowed limbs and a constant, fierce sneer plastered on his face. With his gear on, I wagered he was as wide as he was tall. He also sported a bleached yellow faux-hawk—a terrible look for a man as consumed with courting the opposite sex as Junk was. But Junk didn't give a shit, and that was why we got along.

Junk stopped at what I was sure he deemed a safe, manly distance away from me. He spat a few sunflower seeds onto the mound. I could feel his earthy, brown eyes searching my face for clues.

"Hawk," he said at last.

My nickname sounded as familiar to my ears as my own name. I touched the bill of my cap in reply. He smiled, revealing the gap between his two front teeth I'd gotten so accustomed to seeing over the years.

"You're thinking about all the tang we're going to get back at school when they hear we're going to the championship, right?"

I took off my hat and brushed away some imaginary sweat on my forehead with the back of my glove. The leather was velvety smooth from constant use. The hide was a thicker version of my own skin, something I'd always envied.

"Not exactly," I said.

He nodded as if he could read my mind. I doubted he'd be so hopeful if he could. The pages in my head were filled with dark deeds and wicked thoughts. I'd once called my dying mother a bitch because she didn't let me get a letter jacket like the rest of the guys on the team had. Granted, sixteen year-old me hadn't known how expensive chemo was, but I wasn't expecting a *get out of bad luck free* pass from the karma police to show in my inbox anytime soon.

"You're nervous, I get that. You're running a perfect game—that'd make any pitcher sack-up. We're up one to nothing, and all you need to do is throw two strikes to get us to the show." He slapped me on the shoulder and shifted his weight from foot to foot in a near-prance. "The fucking show, Ernie."

I offered him a sly smile. "Guess it's a pretty big deal, huh?"

He laughed and punched me on the arm. The entire stadium would've died to know what we were talking about.

Truthfully, that was one of the best-kept secrets in all of baseball. A catcher-pitcher conference rarely had a damn thing to do with the game. The act was more of a mental ballet instigated by the catcher. The two personalities would move in a highly choreographed routine to elicit a desired look or feeling from the pitcher.

Confidence. Calm. Determination. That was what a catcher wanted to see from his pitcher before he went back behind the plate. If he didn't, the coach usually came out to yank the pitcher. Most catchers thought pitchers weren't aware of this game of calm-you-down, but Junk knew that I knew better. He'd always said that was why I was such a great pitcher. I had insight.

Honestly, I wasn't sure if Junk even knew what the word meant.

"A pretty big deal? A big deal was *you* convincing Police Chief Janski to let us take his twin daughters to senior prom. A big deal is what I did with Molly Janski in the bed of my pickup truck *after* prom. No my friend, this is nut-busting, change-your-life epic-balls. Two dudes from *Rat's Ass Farming Town*, Illinois, are about to go to Nebraska for the championship series. And you're doing it with a perfect game. Holy shit, Ernie. The national sports reporters are going to be so far up your ass, you'll need surgery and a comfy pillow to get rid of 'em."

This time I laughed. There wasn't any heart in the sound, though. Heart took courage. Nothing courageous about going back on the one promise I'd ever made to the only person I was *sure* loved me. But I needed out of this … this endless cycle of expectations I could never live up to. I'd never been able to find a clear path out of my personal fog. Until today.

"You better get back to home plate before the Walrus comes out," I said.

I glanced at the dugout. The Walrus, or Coach Bo to his face, was definitely glaring at us. The bushy eyebrow and mustache duo were in full scowl mode. I could almost see his thick neck bulging from here. Although I was counting on his hatred for me to usher my exit from the team, and school, I didn't need it right this second.

Junk slid his catcher's mask down. He turned to leave, but paused to look over his shoulder at me.

"You good, Ernie?"

"I'm perfect," I said, my throat so tight the words barely slid out at all.

Leaning over to pick up the rosin bag, I glanced up in enough time to see Junk give the dugout the thumbs up on his way back to home plate.

I'm so sorry, buddy. Mom might have understood that college had been her dream, not mine. She might've even convinced me the scuttling of my college baseball career wasn't my fault. Would Junk understand why I couldn't simply quit instead of taking his dreams, and the dreams of the entire team, down with me like the goddamn Titanic? Somehow, I doubted it.

I took my spot back on the pitching rubber. The crowd roared as the ump waved the batter over. "Play ball."

Arms laced behind my back, I rolled the baseball in my non-gloved hand. There were one hundred and eight red double stitches on the ball, and I touched them all before every pitch. Almost all baseball players have their superstitions, and that was mine. If I missed one, I started over, but I rarely ever missed anything unless I wanted to.

I watched Junk for my pitch. He flashed his fingers in between his legs, giving me a couple of bullshit calls to start, in case the other team was stealing signs. I was pretty sure one of them was meant to be something vulgar. In the end, I shrugged them both off.

The splitter. That was the only pitch to call in this scenario, and we both knew it.

The other team hadn't gotten within the same zip code of my split-finger fastball all day. I could sympathize with them. It couldn't be easy hitting something the size of a fist with a bat when it was flying ninety miles-per-hour from sixty feet away. The task became all that much more difficult when trying to hit a splitter that could drop from chest-height to hitting the ground in the span of a second.

The right call finally came, and I nodded. I brought my arms around in front of me again, covering my ball hand with the mitt. I found the right ball seams with my forefingers and thumb — an almost unconscious act. I focused on the spot where I wanted the ball to end up, which was just behind the plate in the dirt and into Junk's waiting, oversized catcher's glove.

The ambient sound in the stadium went away, replaced by my pulse thundering in my ears. I brought my arms high above my head in an arch, contorting my legs in a visually awkward but physically comfortable pretzel. My jaw locked, making my teeth creak as I drew all of the strength my abdomen and legs would offer. I lunged, unleashing the pitch.

"Strike two!"

The crowd erupted. My stomach tightened. I'd gotten two strikes, so I'd at least put up the front of doing this thing for real. Wouldn't do to get pulled from the game before I completed my mission.

I held up my glove to receive Junk's return pitch. With the ball securely in my mitt, I scanned the small-but-full stadium. Nameless faces cheered and jeered at me. All they could see was a guy who was damned good at baseball. I'm sure they imagined someone who never screwed anything up, someone with the talent to do things they'd only dreamed about. They probably all wanted to be perfect me, in this perfect moment, and experience the perfect ecstasy of the inevitable triumph.

But I knew the truth. Life wasn't perfect, and it could never be. Husbands beat their wives and went to prison. Single mothers died alone, when all they'd ever done to deserve it was work three jobs, make sure their ungrateful kid had a full belly, and give him a chance to get the education she never did. Kids got kicked out of school for not giving a shit about anyone or anything. Boys playing little league for the punch and snacks at the end of the games grew into men who would give anything for one shot at playing for money in the big leagues.

No, life wasn't perfect, and I'd be damned if I'd ever get tricked into believing that lie again. *Face it Ernie, you just can't have nice things.*

I waved off Junk's splitter sign. He paused, and I knew he was suspicious. Another moment, and he gave the sign for a high fastball. I nodded. My control had been flawless all afternoon. I think I could have thrown a fastball into a coffee can at a hundred feet. I was that locked in. But this one wasn't going into a coffee can…

I went through my windup, and flung the ball with all the anger and venom I could muster. I closed my eyes and waited for what felt like an eternity. A split-second later there was a soft-thud followed by the sound of the batter screaming in agony. The crowd gasped.

I'd found my mark.

Chapter Two

The Walrus paced around the empty locker room, muttering expletives and kicking every piece of gear in his path. First, he rocketed a mitt into the side of a trashcan. Then, he toppled a sack of dingy balls over in an avalanche. Finally, he caught a jockstrap with the edge of his shoe and flung it in a wide, floating arch into a urinal. His face cycled through various shades of purple. He still hadn't said a word to me directly.

What was I feeling as I witnessed a middle-aged man throw a tantrum that made the word epic seem small? *Nothing.*

Well, I registered a few things. I felt every drop of cold-water that trickled off my hair to drip onto my bare shoulders, tickling its way over the muscled ridges of my abdomen. The cheap towel wrapped around my waist was soaked through, and chaffed against my skin with every movement. The tile floor might as well have been ice under my feet after exiting the warm shower only a minute or two before. But all of that sensory information was only skin deep.

All the things on the inside, the things that really felt anything, were walled off in a familiar cocoon of *I don't give damn.*

The Walrus charged. His fists clinched into sizeable balls of iron rage. I actually thought he would swing at me, so I flattened my back against the wall and waited for the blow. Our eyes met. I stuck out my chin to take the punishment, not fight back. He pulled up. A man after my own heart ... guess he liked a challenge. All I could muster right then was an aggressive apathy.

I deserved an ass kicking for what I'd done, but the Walrus had too much pride to beat up a punk kid who wouldn't fight back. I was a little disappointed.

Coach Ramirez stepped between us, his leathery brown skin clashing with the white of the Walrus's mustache as he put a forearm across the much larger man's chest to stay him. The Walrus looked at him as if he'd been shaken from a bad dream.

"Fuck." The Walrus spun away from Ramirez and kicked one of the benches that ran down the middle of the narrow room.

It was the first thing he'd struck that didn't move. I didn't know if that defeated him or what, but he collapsed on the seat and ran his hands through his snowy hair over and over.

"Maybe it's best if we take the bus ride home to cool down," Coach Ramirez said in his pleasantly thick Spanish accent. "Give Ernie time to explain his side of things. I'm sure—"

"No." The Walrus's voice was strained, coming out like

the forced growl of a jungle cat. "I want answers. Now. That boy cost his team—his community—a chance at something they've dreamed of their entire lives. He owes them that much."

I let my head bounce against the concrete wall behind me, creating more feeling, but still not the important kind. The inside kind.

Coach Ramirez sighed. "Ernie, what *did* happen out there? You were rocking and rolling, *hermano*. Then, *nada*. You hit a batter and gave up a homerun on the next pitch. That's not the Ernie I know. Nerves?"

The Walrus laughed.

"Bullshit it was nerves. He doesn't give a damn about anyone or anything. This was another opportunity for him to show up his coach. I haven't forgotten the times you've walked out of team meetings … your blatant disregard for team rules at every turn." He thrust his hand out. "Look at him. He's sitting there stone-faced and freshly showered when some of his teammates were so torn up, they went straight to the bus in their gear. Your buddy Junkyard's eye black was streaked with tears. But you don't care about all that, do you, hotshot?"

I swallowed back a boulder-sized lump in my throat. Junk hadn't even looked at me after the game. No one had. The other team had stormed the field, forcing all of us off in a shameful exodus. Just like that, our team, such an unbreakable bond of brotherhood only moments before, shattered into twenty-eight disillusioned pieces.

A warm tear tickled its way down my cheek and mingled with the cold remnants of shower water. I felt something at last, and it wasn't sweet freedom from being released from the dreams of others, but rather the bitter and unfamiliar taste of failure. I'd failed *everyone*.

Ramirez held up his hand. "Coach, I don't think Ernie—"

"Stop taking up for me." I smacked my palm against the wall. "He's right, okay? I've got no excuse. I did it on purpose."

Ramirez's mouth hung open. "You … you can't mean that, Ernie."

Sniffling out a mirthless chuckle, I said, "I swear, it's like she sent you to chaperone me from the grave. Quit believing in me. You fought so damned hard to get me on this team, did it ever occur to you I might not want to be?"

"You sure took the scholarship," the Walrus snapped.

"I did." I tugged at the damp curls of my hair. "I've regretted it every day since."

"You ungrateful piece of—"

Coach Ramirez cleared his throat loud enough to create a slight echo. "Why didn't you come to me, Ernie? We could've talked about it."

I shrugged. "Guess I felt crushed by the weight of living. Getting booted from the team was the only way I knew how to get out from under it short of … other things."

Ramirez sighed. "We're getting you some help—"

"No. I'm done with him. He's off the team." The Walrus pointed at me. If the finger had been loaded, he'd have shot me dead right there. "No more scholarship. No more rolling around campus like you're the biggest shit in the toilet.

I've put up with your shenanigans long enough. We're not running a home for boys with momma issues. You're officially someone else's problem."

Their eyes swept over every inch of me, one man searching for threads of strength, the other probing for fatal cracks in my armor. They should have been looking for holes. I was full of them.

"I fucked up. I'm sorry." My voice could have been one of those computer generated, phone voice recordings. It was that alien sounding in my own ears.

The Walrus's face went full red. *Time for liftoff.*

He stood and turned his back to me. "Not good enough. You're done. I don't want to see you in the facility the rest of the semester, and I'll run any of your teammates until their mommas puke if they so much as speak your name around me. Bus leaves in fifteen with or without you." He glanced over his shoulder at me. "See? I can *not* care, too."

He exited quickly and quietly, as most violent storms do. I was left a broken mess in his wake. All in one day, I'd stood atop a mountain only to have it crumble underneath me. Brought down by my own hand.

Chapter Three

I hiked across the parking lot, wandering beneath one halogen lamp after another. The golden halos of light they gave off did little to scare away the shadows in my mind. Thoughts of loss and betrayal ate me alive from the inside out. I squeezed my hands open and closed, stabbing the soft flesh of my palms with my nails.

My motorcycle was parked at the far end — a good five hundred yards from where we'd been dropped off — but in the bus, on the trip back, the walk down the aisle to my seat had seemed much longer. Some of the guys had donned their headphones, undoubtedly trying to let the tunes drown out the pain of the loss. Others stared straight ahead, bloodshot eyes boring into the seats in front of them. None of them had looks or words for me.

So I took my quiet spot at the back and read poetry on my phone, like I always did on the bus ride home after games. I'd hoped making the outside appear normal would force the inside to mirror, but that had failed spectacularly with the first poem I pulled up.

It was another Robert Frost called *A Late Walk,* and it was a doozy of a downer about—as far as I could tell—a guy walking through a garden realizing he has screwed up with his girl. One line particularly gnawed at me:

A tree beside the wall stands bare,
But a leaf that lingered brown,
Disturbed, I doubt not, by my thought,
Comes softly rattling down.

Exactly like the poor bastard in the garden, I'd wrecked everything. Not with a girl—thankfully, I'd learned to keep them at a safe distance over the years—but my twisted, fucking brain had shaken the last leaf from a tree I'd been intent on killing my entire life. I was free.

Thing was, now that my mother's dream for me was all but dead, I wanted grab all the leaves and try to put them back on the damned tree. Like a kid trying to convince the little brother he'd punched not to cry, I yearned to undo all of the harm I'd caused my friends, the fans, hell, maybe even to the Walrus. But the adult in me knew better. There was nothing left to do but move on.

And at the heart of it, wasn't that what I'd wanted? To move on? Now, there was nothing keeping me from flying solo. No team. No Junkyard. No expectations. Just me living out my flawed life.

I adjusted the strap on my book bag and stared at the sky as I walked the final few feet to my bike. There were either a million stars out or my eyes were watering so much they turned the single lamp above me into a thousand points of diamond light. In either case, I felt small. And alone.

Note to self: Quit reading Robert Frost when you're highly emotional.

I fished in my pocket until I felt the cold, metal clasp of my keychain. I set my bag down beside the bike and pulled out my helmet. It was black, shiny, and sleek—like my motorcycle. The cycle was about the only thing I owned in the world. I'd bought it with the little bit of insurance money that had come to me after Mom died.

A solution sped into my consciousness as I wrapped my hand over the throttle. I could put the helmet on the ground, straddle the bike, hit one-hundred-and-twenty MPH in about a block, find the nearest tree or brick wall, and—

"Ernie?"

"Huh?" I spun around, restraining from throwing my helmet on instinct.

Coach Ramirez poked his head out of the driver's side window of a turtle-like hybrid car in the parking lot beside my motorcycle. I hadn't heard him pull up.

"Thought that was you. You okay? Need a lift?"

Still frightened by what I'd been thinking when he'd startled me, I shook my head and fiddled with my helmet.

"Sure? It's been a long day for all of us I think. *Escucha.*"

That was the word he'd use to get our attention in practice. I wasn't sure what it meant, and had always kind of assumed it was a curse word because it was usually followed by curse words I understood. But this time, he said it gently. His eyes were tired and full of worry.

"You're young. You made a mistake—a big one. But we all do, *muchacho.* You'll have better days."

I sighed. "Not so sure about that right now, Coach."

He surprised me with a laugh.

"Life is all about do-overs, Ernie. Look at me. If it weren't for second chances, I wouldn't be with my third wife. That first one didn't count, by the way."

I chuckled, and it felt like something heavy had been moved off my chest, letting the cool, night air in for the first time.

"I talked to Coach Bo. He's still pissed, and frankly, so am I. What you did out there..." He grimaced like he'd swallowed back something sour. "Well, it doesn't matter now. It's done. What matters is that you get help."

I felt my brow furrow. I wasn't seeking a way back in, no matter how shitty I felt about what I'd done. "Look, I—"

He held up his hand to stop me. "I know, I know. Hear me out. It was a hard sell, but we agreed to revisit your scholarship and place on the team. If you get some real help—demonstrate that you've changed—I think I can get you another shot, *hermano*."

I blew out a chest full of air. Coach Ramirez was determined, and I'd tried him enough to know he wasn't likely going to let me ride off into the sunset. And there *was* that stray thought I'd had about becoming one with a tree. There was no arguing I'd taken this a few steps further than simply thumbing my nose at authority and mother's wishes.

"What kind of help?" I pulled my keys out of my pocket.

"There's a counseling center here on campus. They're good people. Helped me get through that second divorce I mentioned. More importantly, they helped me out with the alcohol problem that caused it. They're a little unorthodox."

"Coach, I don't think that's for me. My problems are my problems. The more people I draw into them, the worse it is for everyone. You know what I did today. I can't—"

"¡*Oye!*" He slapped his hand on his steering wheel, causing the horn to chirp. "The Ernie I recruited wouldn't use that word. The Ernie who got us to the gate of the championship series wouldn't use that word. The Ernie who pitched the first six innings of that game wouldn't use that word. You can, and you will. I'll call them and tell them to expect to see you next week."

Coach Ramirez didn't give me a chance to argue. He cranked the volume on whatever Spanish music station he'd dialed up and crept into the night.

Cutting me off with his music was a trick he'd learned to use on me the day I got to campus. I gave him grief about having to cut my hair. Back then, it was almost down to my shoulders. I'd stormed into his office to throw a fit, and he'd pointed to the Five Commandments—the absurdly large list of team rules on the wall behind his desk. Then he sang along to the mariachi music he had blaring 24/7.

He laughed. I was pissed, but ultimately, I buzzed my hair like the rest of the team. Well, everything except for a long stripe down the middle. That, and my predatory disposition toward batters, was how I'd gotten the nickname Hawk.

The Five Commandments looked like something a public swimming pool would have up more than a page out of the Old Testament. But they were so old-fashioned and rigid, the moniker definitely fit: NO FIGHTING - ON OR OFF THE FIELD; NO DRINKING OR DRUGS - ON OR OFF THE FIELD; NO FAILING GRADES AT MIDTERM OR FINALS;

NO PUTTING YOURSELF BEFORE YOUR TEAM; NO HAIR BELOW THE JAWLINE.

With my latest incident, except for the fighting, I'd managed to violate all of them in some fashion in my first two years. College Algebra had nearly killed me, but I'd been smart enough to take the class during the fall semester when there wasn't actual baseball to be missed. I'd gotten my ass chewing at midterm when the Walrus had seen my D-minus and ran a few dozen extra miles at practice for the rest of the semester. But by the end, I'd figured things out and gotten my average up to a high C.

I'd always prided myself on being able to finish strong. Yet lately, all I could think about was giving up.

I slid the helmet over my ears and straddled the bike. The leather seat squeaked underneath my weight as I adjusted for takeoff. I throttled up, relishing the way the engine's roar split the quiet of the night and the noise in my head so efficiently. For the first time all day, I felt a little control and normalcy come back into my life.

Coach Ramirez was right. If I was going to finish my life strong—or at all—I needed help.

Chapter Four

The counseling center—or Fredrick House, as the building was so labeled on the campus map—was hidden away behind the President's House. Could have been a coincidence. Maybe it was the last free building on campus. But there was still something of a closed-door mentality when came to mental illness in my part of the world. According to some of the old Midwestern farmers I'd encountered, *normal* people didn't go to shrinks. They damn sure didn't take pills to make them happy. That kind of stuff belonged to the Hollywood types.

I had news for the farmers: there wasn't anything glitzy about the cornfields of Southern Illinois, and I was pretty sure the cows weren't taking all those happy pills.

I spent five minutes winding the path around the hedges and a modest rose garden, to the side yard. Once there, an even more expansive lawn greeted me. Several large fountains gurgled at various clearings in the distance. I assumed the counseling center would be somewhere in the back, where a row of trees and a giant hedge formed a vibrant green wall. Naturally, I got lost. I'd followed one of the hedge trails that looked promising, but ended up next to a storage shed near the main house. Then, I bumped into Willy.

The rake jutting from his hand had more teeth than he did. One of his eyes had gone from being lazy to full on asleep, giving him this kind of permanent, toothless sneer. I asked if I was going in the right direction. He cackled and threw his hands into the air. It was a weird, half-delighted, half-shocked gesture — like I'd offered to dance with him, and then said I would set the place on fire when we were done fox-trotting.

He eventually quit wheezing long enough to say, "You're plum going the wrong direction, honey. Dis here the president's kitchen entrance. Less'n you able to cook up a mess of those cupcakes he fancies, you ain't likely to git in dare."

I smiled as he stamped his rake up and down to the rhythm of another fit of laughter.

"Ol' Willy jus' pullin' yo chain, honey. You jus' keep on going back through the garden dare. Gate'll take you where you want to go, I 'spect."

I turned to leave Willy to his *freaking-random-passers-by-the-hell-out* , and he caught my arm. I eyed him calmly but really considered running away like a frightened puppy.

"Sure you want to go dare? They some strange folk up in dat house. You seem like a normal one to me. Even stopped to talk to Ol' Willy a spell."

That word again. Normal, not normal — if there were a baseline for human existence, I'd never found it in anyone.

I smiled again, and patted him on the arm. "Afraid my normal is only skin-deep, Willy. Thanks for your help."

He nodded, and I made my way through the garden.

The outside looked like something that inspired the cheesy paintings I'd seen on decorative plates sold in truck stops. There was a small front porch with two rocking chairs, and a simple gold-trimmed placard on one of the porch beams read: Fredrick House.

I took a small step backward. I'd found the counseling office, now all I wanted to do was put it behind me. While I knew Coach Ramirez truly wanted to help me, I also knew he was angling for me to get back on the team and stay in school. My agenda was the opposite, so what *was* I hoping to accomplish here?

A voice in my head, sounding eerily similar to one my mother had used when she'd explain why I needed to take out the trash, said, "You're here so you don't kill yourself, stupid."

Point awarded: Mom.

A bell above the front door jangled, announcing my entrance. Dangling from a rusty nail next to a downward stairwell, a sign read: *I'm not crazy. My reality is different than yours.*

I grinned in spite of my wary mood. Another set of stairs went up. I could at least see some light up there, so that's where I went.

Odors of coffee and cinnamon saturated the air. All the overdone touches of home made me a little itchy. I stood in front of the receptionist's desk, except the girl sitting behind it didn't look like much of a receptionist. The hair poking out from the bottom of her beanie hat was dyed raven black with crimson streaks. Her T-shirt was turned inside out, but I could still make out the word *motherfucker* embossed underneath it.

"Excuse me."

She bobbed her head up and down—like maybe she had some kind of nervous disorder—as she stared at her phone. Her fingers tapped the screen so quickly and rhythmically, I half-believed she could only be typing the same word over and over. Without breaking eye contact with her phone, she snatched an absurdly large can of energy drink off the desk and chugged. After a small belch, she went right back to ignoring me and moving her head.

I cleared my throat. "I have an appointment."

Still no response, so I figured I was out of her line of sight and stepped forward.

She glared at me, and her cat-eyes narrowed like she might be ready to pounce. "What?"

I frowned. "An appointment. I have one. With a counselor, I guess."

She rolled her eyes and tugged earbuds out of her ears. "Did you sign in?"

I offered my best *don't fuck with me* look—one I usually reserved for ballsy batters who crowded home plate—but she didn't blink. She'd make one hell of a pitcher.

I sighed. "Okay, let's try again. I don't know what I'm doing here. In fact, I'm not even sure I want to be here. A little help?"

She pointed to an area behind my head with her non-phone hand. "Sign in. I'll let Dr. Jones know you're here."

Amidst an area of mismatched chairs and small tables, I found a clipboard with names and times scrawled on it. I jotted my signature on a free line and plopped down in a wingback with pink roses on it. Halfway through a pamphlet on Seasonal Affective Disorder—apparently some people were *really* into sunshine—the angry receptionist told me I could go back to the office, except I had no idea where it was.

I grabbed the handle to the door closest to me.

"That's a closet," Angry said, the dry sarcasm in her tone giving the dust I imagined hiding in the rafters of this place a run for its money.

Instead of responding, I searched the room and saw a door partially hidden behind a massive wreath bedecked with crimson and gold ribbons—our school colors. I went straight for it, not giving the receptionist a second look on the way by. *What a hag.*

As I let myself in, Angry said, "You're not special, you know."

Perfect.

"Thanks for that," I said, wishing sarcasm could cause bodily injury. "You've been very helpful."

"No, I … I mean no one is sure they want to be here, but they usually need to be here. That's all I meant."

Holy shit. Even the people who work here are crazy.

"Have a seat wherever you'd like," Dr. Jones, presumably, said to me as I made my way across the room toward her desk.

I diverted mid-path to a comfy-looking leather sofa lined up against a far wall. The couch was stationed strategically between the door and the doctor. I had no desire to be trapped if things went south.

Dr. Jones grabbed a notepad off her desk and moved in my direction. She was dressed in a calf-length turquoise skirt and white blouse. Her hair, black with sprinkles of gray, fell around her reading glasses in springy curls.

She smiled and adjusted her glasses before sitting on a nearby ottoman. "Tell me a little about yourself, Ernest."

The inquisition begins.

I adjusted in my seat, straightening my posture. "You can call me Ernie."

"Good. Tell me a little about yourself, *Ernie.*"

She stared at me over the top of her glasses that had once again slid down her nose. What would a counselor want to know about me? I had that kind of stuff running out of my goddamned ears. Might as well let her have it with both barrels.

"My dad beat my mother and went to prison when I was five. He got out, robbed a gas station, and killed the attendant on the same day, then went back for good. Mom died of cancer two years ago. I have no siblings, no living grandparents, and my only aunts and uncles are on Dad's side of the family. I hate them, and they hate me. It works. I came to school here on a baseball scholarship but recently found myself separated from the team for conduct unbecoming a baseball player on scholarship. I did it on purpose, because I really don't want to be in college."

She smiled dismissively, as if she'd heard these kinds of bad luck stories every day.

"That's unfortunate, but I was thinking more along the lines of what's your favorite food and what you do when you're not playing baseball—or begrudgingly going to college."

I didn't see how that kind of stuff mattered much in counseling, but I figured I'd play along.

"Okay, I really love sushi. Like, *I-can-eat-all-of-it-in-the-world* love it. I read a lot, but I really enjoy riding my motorcycle when I've got nothing else to do."

"Sushi? Now *that's* interesting. How'd a Midwestern kid like you acquire a taste for sushi?"

"Mom always talked about how much she loved sushi. But I never saw her eat it—not once. Which I thought was the weirdest thing as a kid. I mean, I loved pizza, and I made sure I ate it at every turn. Anyway, when I got to college, I went on the long baseball trips and ate at fancier places. The team paid for everything, so if I saw sushi on the menu, that's what I ordered. Just trying to figure out why Mom enjoyed it so much. Honestly, the texture grossed me the hell out the first few times I had it. But I eventually got to where I craved it."

Outside of the window across the room, a hummingbird greedily sucked nectar from a feeder suctioned to the glass.

"It sounds silly to say it now, but I never realized until after she was gone why she didn't eat it," I said, not certain what had provoked me to add that part.

"And why do you think that was?" Her tone indicated she might have already known the answer but was interested in hearing it come from me.

I ran my hands over my head. "She didn't eat it so I could have pizza. Sushi was too expensive, so she sacrificed what she wanted so I could have the things I enjoyed. Looking back, she did that kind of stuff all the time."

"And how does that make you feel?"

I laughed. "I should say grateful. But truthfully, it pisses me off. To the point I sometimes fucking hate her for it. She didn't get much life to begin with. She shouldn't have wasted what she was given on me. She should've taken care of herself. I never asked for that kind of attention. The only way I could think of to repay her was to go to college, and that hasn't gone so well, either."

I slapped my hand down on the leather sofa. When I finally looked at Dr. Jones again, I expected to see a frown or some other indication of disapproval. Instead, she scribbled on her notepad and gave me a soft smile.

"Have you had any thoughts of harming yourself?"

I threw my head back and groaned. "Yes."

"Have you formulated a plan to do it?"

"No ... not really."

"How *not really?*" she asked, her eyes narrowing.

"I don't know. It was a stupid idea when I was upset."

Saying that I'd considered crashing my bike aloud suddenly felt too real—like admitting a nightmare was more than a bad dream. Those kinds of declarations could be dangerous to a fragile mind, and mine was as thin as porcelain at the moment.

"Ernie, if I'm going to help you, I need you to be honest with me. You can say anything here, it won't—"

I stood. "I thought about wrapping myself around a tree. Only for a second, but it was there. It scared me. That's the reason why I came here. What's one more mistake heaped on the pile I've made recently?"

"With time, we can work through this," Dr. Jones said, standing with me.

I went to the door. "I think I already have, Doc. You can't help me. No one can."

Chapter Five

Book reliquary, mausoleum of information, boring—I'd heard libraries called all kinds of unflattering names. For me, the old tomes were a fountain of youth, and the quiet nooks, a sanctuary from the chaos of my mind. I could pull a collection of poetry from the shelf, pop on my headphones, and set the mental cruise control for a few hours. I'd always end up in a better place. That's where I went after my counseling session.

I hadn't thought so when I'd left, but Dr. Laura had shaken me. With a few simple questions, she'd stomped on a raw nerve. Now, I only had to decide if that was good thing or not.

What *does* one read when feeling mildly suicidal and *very* melancholic?

I chose the collected work of Sir Alfred, Lord Tennyson. Published at seventeen, he was forced to leave Cambridge—where he was an ace student—before getting his degree to help care for his widowed mother and family. His second poetry collection was so slammed by critics, he didn't publish again for a decade. He only went on to be best buds with the Royal Family and one of the most decorated poets of all time. Driven, optimistic, a dedicated family man and friend — if he were a poet superhero, I might be his brooding archenemy.

No, I had the distinct feeling Big Al wouldn't put up with my bullshit if he were around today. *Ernest, why doth thou protest like a twaddling child? Go forth! Seize the virtuous day!*

The book was large enough, I decided to take over the musty loveseat in the back corner of the poetry section. I kicked off my shoes and draped my legs over the arm. At nearly six feet, four inches, the couch was more like a big chair. Anyway, this was dinnertime at the cafeteria, so I knew I'd have the place mostly to myself.

Resting the hardback on my stomach, I flipped through the pages, tapping my fingers to the beat of a classic *Strokes* tunes. I quickly found a winner:

Ask Me No More

Ask me no more: the moon may draw the sea;
The cloud may stoop from heaven and take the shape,
With fold to fold, of mountain or of cape;
But O too fond, when have I answer'd thee?
Ask me no more.

Ask me no more: what answer should I give?
I love not hollow cheek or faded eye:
Yet, O my friend, I will not have thee die!
Ask me no more, lest I should bid thee live;
Ask me no more.

Ask me no more: thy fate and mine are seal'd:

I strove against the stream and all in vain:
Let the great river take me to the main:
No more, dear love, for at a touch I yield;
Ask me no more.

I'd been swimming up stream my entire life. And for what? Two years of college felt like a waste. If the pro scouts talked to the Walrus, was he likely to give me a glowing endorsement? Doubtful. My only real friends were on the team, but if word got out that I'd thrown the game on purpose, I couldn't see many of them showing at my next birthday party. The demands of life had left me exhausted. Maybe the time had come to go with the flow and let the river take me where it would…

Someone brushed my leg.

"Sorry," I said, not really looking.

I figured my body was sticking out too far, so I scrunched my all the way onto the couch. I flipped through a few more pages. Another brush came, but it was more of an insistent tap this time.

"Yeah?" I asked, laying the book in my lap.

A girl wearing a floral dress, sneakers, and a lavender cardigan looked down on me from the end of the couch. Her lips and cheeks were an identical shade of sunset pink, the former moving quickly.

"Forgot I had these on." I slipped my headphones off. "What's up?"

"I was curious." She offered me a tight-lipped smile. A ponytail of curly red hair swayed behind her. "How much longer are you planning on using that book?"

Her arms were folded over her torso, her hips jutted slightly to one side.

I shrugged. "Just started with it. Might be a while."

She adjusted a set of thick-rimmed glasses with a wrinkle of her nose. "I really need it."

I laughed a little too loudly for being in a library. She startled.

"Sorry, it's just that I can't imagine anyone needing it more than me right now."

Her gaze drifted to my torso. My shirt had ridden up, revealing my abs. I smiled at her and she flushed. She was pretty, in a huffy, confrontational sort of way.

Her eyes rolled slightly. I wasn't sure if she was more exasperated with herself or me.

"I've got a big day tomorrow, and I *really* have to have that book."

I scratched my chin, pretending to think. There was no reason I couldn't pull up poems on my phone, or find another book. Still, so could she. And I *hated* being bossed around.

"I'll leave it out when I'm done."

Her hands went to her hips. "I'm sure you think hanging out in libraries, pretending to read poetry, is a great way to pick up chicks—or whatever it is baseball players are doing for giggles these days. But some of us are here to actually learn and require this information to do so."

Realizing I was wearing one of my team T-shirts, and that she hadn't been checking me out earlier, embarrassed me more than I was insulted by her basically calling me an athletic chimpanzee. I hid my stomach with the book. I'd dealt with her type before. Jocks weren't supposed to read, think, or eat with utensils.

I put my feet on the ground. "What makes you so sure I don't *require* this as much as you? Maybe I've got a paper to work on?"

It was her turn to laugh too loudly. "I'm quite familiar with the English department. I'm pretty sure you don't. Anyway, Isn't there a team *tutor* who'd do it for you?"

Well-played, overly presumptive and judgmental stranger.

"Not that it's your business, but poetry is really important to me. My mother…"

I realized she was standing there, eyebrows arched, waiting for me to finish. But I couldn't. At last, I'd found a way I hadn't let my mother down.

I pushed the book into her arms and took off at a trot. Halfway to the stairs, I remembered I wasn't wearing my shoes. She watched me as I ran back, a confused grin on her face. Dangling my flip-flops from one hand, I patted her on the shoulder with the other.

"Thanks for being such a pain in the ass," I said.

She frowned.

"No seriously, thank you. You're a lifesaver."

When I made it back to the counseling center, Dr. Laura was on the porch holding her briefcase.

"Hey, Doc." I hoped I sounded less silly than I felt. "Got a second?"

"Sure." She sat in one of the rocking chairs and offered me the other. "Here, sit down."

I did, and pretended to inspect the wood on the arm of the chair. I knew why I'd come back, but now that I was here, saying I needed help seemed stupid and obvious. "I was afraid I'd miss you."

"I'm sorry your session ended like it did. Is everything alright?"

"It's great. Well, not great, or I wouldn't be here. Right?" I laughed, but the sound played more nervous than jovial in my ears. *Quit stalling, Ernie.* "I realize it's only been a few hours since I saw you, and this is going to sound crazy, but I figured something out."

Her face brightened with a smile. "Not as crazy as you might think. Tell me."

"Poetry. It's always been the poetry."

"I'm not sure I'm following—"

"Mom loved to read, especially poetry." I stood and paced the porch. "She'd always recite me some before bedtime and when I'd get nervous before games. After she died, her old books were all I really kept."

"Reading poetry was a way of memorializing her."

"Right, and I've never stopped. In fact, I love it now. Like the sushi, but this is actually important."

Dr. Laura chuckled. "It is important. And special. You think she'd be proud of you for this, correct?"

I nodded. "I do. Even after all I've done wrong, she'd love this about me."

"You seem to have reached some sort of conclusion from all of this."

"I did." I sat back down. "I found something worth salvaging in me, Doc. If there's one thing, there has to be more. Would you still be willing to help me? I won't ever storm out again."

She offered me an apologetic smile. "You can definitely find help here, but I'm not sure I'm exactly the right person to give it to you, Ernie."

"Wait ... what?" I flinched. After the last few days, I knew I'd been kidding myself earlier. This might be the *only* place on campus I belonged. And I'd swallowed too much pride coming back to her to be shot down. "I'm no counselor, but I think things are going really well. Isn't this what you'd call a breakthrough?"

"Oh, it's not a matter of it going poorly. I think we're getting on fabulously, and it's certainly a breakthrough. I'm not sure we'd get to where you need to go with just the two of us."

I grabbed the arms of my chair. "I don't care about the team, if that's what you mean. I need to get better."

She patted my arm. "Ernie, relax. I didn't say we couldn't help you. I simply don't think individual counseling is the best form of treatment. I'm going to recommend you also attend Neyle's weekly group counseling sessions."

"Neyle?"

She rummaged in a bag next to her chair. I took the business card she offered me. A ukulele and a pineapple were embossed on it. I'm sure the look I gave her could've been archived somewhere between *are you shitting me* and *thanks, but no thanks.*

"Neyle uses some unorthodox methods ... ones I certainly wouldn't use. But he's effective in unique cases. I think you're one of those."

I studied her. There was a quiet confidence in her gaze, and a beckoning assuredness in the way she leaned toward me. Almost like a parent encouraging their child to take their first dive off the board at the pool.

"You seriously think he can fix me?"

Dr. Jones shook her head. "I think you can fix you. He's going to show you how. You'll find the group counseling meeting times on the back of the card. And a date for our next appointment."

Had she planned on me coming back all along? She knew me better than me already, and I was beginning to see she how deceptively clever she was, too. I liked her.

"Will we still get to talk?" I asked, hearing a little of the worry in my voice.

"You bet. Someone has to keep an eye on Neyle for me."

Chapter Six

I cracked the classroom door, fully expecting to hear my English professor, Dr. Ben, droning on about assonance making an ass of us all. *My God did that man hate rhyming poetry.* But there was only silence. I swung the door all the way open. The room was empty.

What the hell? I pulled my cellphone out of my pocket to check the time—still a full quarter until eight. I groaned. Guess I'd jumped the gun a little. I had a lot more free time now that I was banned from working out with the team in the mornings.

I headed toward my usual spot in the back corner near the only window. The guys from the team who had the class with me thought I liked to sit back there so we could goof off. They were wrong. I sat there because it was the closest I could get to actually being outside.

I spotted the girl from the library halfway to my seat. She held a stack of papers in one hand and scribbled notes on the whiteboard with the other. Her back was to me, and I said something stupid, like, "We meet again." Then I saw the headphone chords dangling from below the curls of her hair and felt like an idiot. She obviously couldn't hear me.

What was she doing here? Maybe Dr. Ben had asked her to put the lesson up for the day. She struck me as someone who would be a world-class ass kisser, so why not?

I watched her work. Letting her believe she was alone should have made me turn away with voyeuristic shame. But I couldn't *not* look. Observing her was like seeing an expressionist painting come to life. In her ruffled sleeveless blouse, tinted a glimmering shade of lavender, she was all color and shape. She moved in a disjointed yet strangely efficient way, like a bee hovering chaotically from flower to flower.

I smirked each time she'd stretch her long freckled arms to write at the top of the board. There was plenty of room on either side to write, but she seemed hell bent on making things flow her way. Her full hips twitched slightly beneath a knee-length black dress in time with whatever music she listened to.

"Fuck," she said, quickly wiping a misspelled word away with the side of her hand. One of her earbuds yanked free with the flurry of her movement. "Damn it."

I laughed.

She spun on me with a start. "You're early. It's you … from the library."

I pinched my arm. "Yep, definitely me."

Her eyes widened as she gave her watch a panicked glance. "Oh hell, I forgot to make copies of the handout." She sprinted from the room.

And they think I have issues?

After taking my seat, I pulled our class poetry book from my messenger bag and thumbed through the pages. Eventually, I landed in a section about the Metaphysical Movement. The poets of that time quit writing about religion and focused on nature and love, among other things, which I found curious, because I supposed I'd always viewed them as intertwined things.

A few lines from Henry Vaughn jumped out at me, but for different reasons.

I saw eternity the other night,
Like a great ring of pure and endless light

Dr. Ben would *really* hate that one. But, as the campus came to life with students scurrying over the lawns below me, the next line struck me.

They are all gone into the world of light!
And I alone sit ling'ring here;

Was it possible to be at the same school, sitting in the same classroom, and hearing the same droning hum of the fluorescent lights, yet still be on an entirely different plane of existence than those around me? Could I be alive and still somehow be left behind? Lately, I'd thought so.

"Careful, y'all. We got us a psycho on the loose." David Goldstein, our boulder-sized third baseman, sauntered toward me with his dimpled chin sticking out. I liked to picture his face as a target, and the dimple as a bull's-eye I'd one day get to put my fist into.

He wasn't an asshole. He was *the* asshole that puckered all other assholes that dared to squat before him.

"Knock it off," Junk said coming up behind him.

Travis Bashaw trailed Junk and David. He was a skinny relief pitcher on the team who we called Bash. I couldn't recall him ever getting a hit—not even on a bunt. But he threw a lot of strikes. Bash was also my best friend on the team, aside from Junk.

They took the three seats nearest me as the rest of the class wandered in.

Junkyard turned to me. "True they got you seeing a shrink now?"

I nodded and stiffened my jaw to absorb whatever Junk might hit me with next. I'd sent him a couple of texts and hadn't gotten a reply. Not anything out of the ordinary really, because Junk's cell phone was usually in his gym locker or at some girl's dorm room—anywhere but on him. But I hadn't talked to him since the game and didn't really know what the rest of the team had heard. Or more importantly, believed.

He frowned. "Man, that's some bullshit. We all know you aren't crazy or anything."

"No way. We're behind you, Ernie," Bash said, twisting his flat-brimmed hat around backward and nodding grimly.

At least I had the world's least intimidating gangster-wannabe and my best friend on my side. Now if I could only *not* feel like a scumbag.

"Not all of us," David said, furrowing his bushy red eyebrows and crossing his meaty arms.

Junk spun on him. "I thought I told you to ice it with that stuff?"

"Just messing with my teammate. Right, Ernie? You *are* still on the team aren't you?" David's threatening tone betrayed his smile.

He knows damned well Coach suspended me.

There was history between us, and it wasn't the fun, *man lands on the moon* kind. Our past was a bit more of complicated, like, Native Americans and the United States government kind of complicated. Our rivalry started in high school when I struck David out three times in the state regionals. We hadn't been teammates then. Once we were playing together in college, David despised me because I'd been given a scholarship and he'd been forced to walk on his freshman year. The icing on his little hate cupcake had come when I'd gotten the entire team in trouble earlier this season. In my defense, me turning in a bag of syringes I'd found on the team bus to Coach Ramirez was an act of blind naiveté. We had a guy with diabetes, what else was I supposed to think? Turned out, steroids were also delivered by injection. A month of extra sprints after practice, and the coaches still never got anyone to fess up. But that didn't stop David from calling me a nark.

"Don't worry. Me and some of the other guys are gonna talk to him. We'll demand you get reinstated," Junk said.

Oh God, he doesn't know. My head suddenly hurt.

"Don't do that. I'll be fine."

"It's not right. You had a bad game and let the pressure get to you," Bash said.

Junk studied me. "Hell, we've all been there. For him to kick you off the team for it—and then make you go through some bullshit psycho-evaluation-thing on top of that … well, I don't want to play for a guy who'd do that to his best player. It's not like you did it on purpose."

I looked away from him to gaze out the window again. Would he want to play *with* a guy who had intentionally pissed away his team's chance at glory, all because he couldn't distinguish between his happy place and hell? I doubted it.

"Maybe let it cool awhile. Some time away from it all might do me good," I said, marveling at how alien my voice sounded bouncing off the glass.

A silence wedged between us, as if someone had pounded it there with a hammer. Like a kind of psychic clockwork, I could practically hear Junk's thoughts grinding in his head. I'd never given up on anything this easily in my life, and when authority pushed on me, I tended to shove back. Hard. In his eyes, I'm sure this was the equivalent of me curling up in a ball and letting the bear maul me, trusting I'd somehow survive. I felt like Junk was starting to doubt me for the first time ever, and it hurt.

The sick feeling of betrayal soured my stomach and made my bones ache, but I had to keep taking my bitter medicine and hope I didn't infect anyone else with my unique type of madness.

"Whatever." He rummaged in his bag.

Bash clapped me on the shoulder. David huffed.

The library prude turned cursing teacher's aide strolled back into class with a worn leather portfolio tucked underneath one arm and a coffee travel mug in her hand. On the surface, the look—combined with her pixy-featured face—was one I'd normally attribute to someone trying to create a false sense of maturity. Sort of like a kid clomping around in her mom's oversized high heels and dragging her dad's heavy briefcase behind her pretending to be a big girl. But, as she surveyed the room from behind an ancient wooden lectern, I recognized a burning determination in her eyes and an aggressive slant to her posture. On the surface, she appeared to be throwing to shadows in her backyard, imagining they were big leaguers. But something told me she'd put the first pitch next to your chin if she thought you were a real challenge.

I'll be damned if the combined effect wasn't the most attractive thing I'd ever seen in a woman. But it still didn't help me understand what she was doing here. Was she subbing? I was an English minor and hadn't seen her before, so I was pretty sure she wasn't faculty. Not that I would complain. She was much easier on the eyes than bushy-browed Dr. Ben.

"Good morning," she said with only a trace of authority.

It didn't garner more than a few odd glances from those in mid-conversation. I stretched out my legs, curious to see how she would play being ignored.

"Dr. Ben had a heart attack."

Sharp and direct, her words cut through the commotion. This girl knew how to get down to business. She took a bold step in front of the lectern. "I … I'm sorry to bear such bad news."

"Did he die?"

"Is class canceled?"

"Will we get credit for what we've done?"

"Do we all get As?"

She held her hand up to halt the questions.

"The doctors believe Dr. Ben will make a full recovery. Unfortunately, he'll miss the rest of the semester. Class will continue as scheduled—and as outlined in the syllabus—under my direction."

I massaged my face. This was a horrible dream. Had to be. My new teacher couldn't be the person I'd pissed off only yesterday. *Why couldn't you have given her the freaking book, Ernie?*

"My name is Margery—"

David thrust his hand into the air. "Dr. Margery, I may need some *special* instruction." He winked at Junkyard.

"It's *Ms.* Price, not doctor, and definitely not Dr. Margery. You can check with the department office if you need extra help."

"You're not a doctor?"

"No, I'm a graduate student in the fine arts program. I've been Dr. Ben's assistant all year."

"When did the college start using graduate teaching assistants?" a girl in the front row asked.

Ms. Price blushed. "We didn't, technically speaking. This is a special circumstance. I'm familiar with your work and the course. You're in good hands, I assure you."

"I'd like to get familiar with her alright." David made an obscene gesture with his hands, eliciting some dumb laughter from a couple of the guys around us.

"Would it kill you to *not* act like a douchebag for once in your life?" I whispered.

"Lighten up. Just having a little fun—"

Ms. Price cleared her throat. "Gentleman in the back corner, is there a problem?"

I hung my head. If I'd been an irritating blip on her radar before, I was about to become a full-blown object of her scorn.

"We're fine," I said, wishing the word translated to: David is choking on his own tongue.

"No problem, ma'am," David said with a mock salute.

The rest of the hour went smoother, probably because David dozed off.

I waited for the rest of the class to filter out before collecting my things. Ms. Price stuffed papers into her portfolio until her gaze found me. Her eyes were a vibrant, mossy green.

She scowled, and I tightened my grip on the strap of my bag.

"How can I help you?" she asked, but it sounded more like *I hope you taste good, because I'm about to take a bite out of your ass.*

"I wanted to talk to you about what happened at the library yesterday — and class earlier."

"Let's see." Her eyes narrowed as her finger went to her chin. "What was it you called me? Oh, yes, *pain in the ass.*"

I ran my hand over my hair. "Did I say that? I get a little hangry sometimes — "

"Hangry?"

"You know, angry when I'm hungry."

"You expect me to believe your calling me a name had to do with you missing taco night in the cafeteria?"

I scrunched my shoulders. "Yes?"

Her face twitched, like she might be about the smile, but she resumed focusing on her paperwork before I could tell. "And what about you and your teammates disrupting my class? Let me guess, they were all out of Fruity O's this morning."

"I don't even like cereal ... that wasn't my fault by the — "

"Sounded like it from up here." She snapped the latch shut on her bag. "Listen, I was probably out of line at the library myself. But I'll stick to my message: I'm not going to put up with a bunch of crap from people who aren't interested in learning."

I could feel my jaw stiffening but tried to remember why I'd stopped to talk to her in the first place. I needed to make peace with my new instructor. But, man, she knew how to push my buttons.

"You don't know anything about me other than I play baseball." I tugged at the straps of my bag. "What makes you so sure I don't want to learn?"

She crossed her arms. "I've had a front row seat when it comes to student athletes. The baseball players on this campus might be treated like hyper-masculine gods of awesome everywhere else, but in my classroom you'll be held to the same standards as the rest of the students. That clear?"

"As glass," I said and left.

Chapter Seven

Hints of lavender and spice — this basement didn't smell much like a basement. I brushed through the sparkling bead curtain covering the doorway and spotted the source of the odors. A tendril of stale smoke snaked in the air above an incense burner. I stifled a cough with the back of my hand and surveyed my group counseling room with a mixture of bemusement and nagging uncertainty.

A desk huddled against a far wall had a sign taped above it that read: *Hi, my name is Neyle, but you can call me Neal.* There were no chairs in the room, save for the one behind the desk, only cushions — of every shape, color, and size — tossed indiscriminately about. Bookcases lined the white cinderblock walls, and motivational posters papered the visible areas. But there was something off about them.

I inspected the piece of laminated wisdom nearest me. A guy was dangling from the side of a cliff by one arm and stretching toward the sky with the other. The giant word over the picture read FAITH. The original line of inspiration was, *"Is stretching beyond the reach of your grasp, and believing you won't fall!*" But someone had drawn a line through the phrase with a red dry erase marker and wrote, *"Is bullshit if you're trying to kill yourself anyway."*

I chuckled and moved to the next.

DETERMINATION was written above a photo of a woman running a race on two artificial limbs. *"Is mind over body!"* *Is making it through your 8 AM biology lab with a hangover.*

"One of Neyle's class projects. It's surprisingly fun."

I turned and found a guy in oversized round glasses texting with one hand and tossing cushions to the center of the room with the other. He flung a pillow down at his feet and collapsed onto it. After stuffing his phone into his urban camouflaged book bag, he pulled out a laptop covered in stickers. While he waited for the machine to boot, he watched me. His eyes bulged behind thick lenses, making me feel like I was being studied under twin microscopes.

When his gaze finally got too uncomfortable for me to stand, I cleared my throat. "I'm Ernie."

He nodded and returned his attention to his computer. "Name is Lex, but my gamer tag is Luther. You can call me either."

"Cool," I mumbled and snagged my own cushion to place next to him. "What's this Neyle guy like?"

"Insane," Luther replied with a creepy, knowing grin. The way his dark skin turned green in the glow of his computer screen conjured images of his super villain namesake.

"Perfect." I crossed my legs and stared at the ceiling.

Soon, a girl joined us. Tiny black pigtails jutted from her head like antennae. She set to work ordering the cushions into a perfect circle around the room, then paused long enough to glare at Luther. "You're such a pig."

"Hey Sing," Luther said over the clicking of his keyboard, completely unaffected.

The ant-like girl straightened her starched cardigan after each flurry of movement, and I seriously questioned my sanity for the first time. This was my peer group now. This was how I appeared to the outside world. Awesome.

The steady stream of newcomers was all that kept me from slinking back out into the night. A stunning, golden-haired girl entered next. She spoke to no one, but smiled a hell of a lot. She sat and applied layers of lip gloss with a care and precision I imagined Michelangelo might have admired.

"That's Abbey," Luther whispered.

There was a reverence in his tone that made me smile — like we were all watching the last unicorn prance before us.

Then came Baker. His hair was pulled back in a ponytail, and he had a hard plastic case tucked under one of his arms. Trumpet maybe, but I didn't know my band instruments. As he sidled next to me, I understood what the incense was for. A thick, pungent aroma trailed him into the room. I'd never smoked, but the smell was familiar enough.

He leaned around me to speak to Luther. "Dude, were you on last night?"

"Of course," Luther said, not looking at him. "We had clan practice. I'm Clan Leader, remember?"

"Right..." Baker blinked heavily as if waking from a nap. "We had some babes over and partied a little. Sorry, bro." He laughed.

Luther frowned. "You're lucky you're one of our best players. Try to make the next one."

"Fully," Baker said and laughed again.

Neyle was the last to arrive. Or at least the man I assumed was Neyle. He had a thick coat of tidy white hair perched atop his head and a matching mustache. His cheeks were full and pink. The loud Hawaiian shirt he wore clashed with his tan Dockers. He wasn't an old man, but he walked with a three-legged cane with a fold out platform that could be used as a stool.

"Hey y'all," he said.

"Hey," the group, minus me, mumbled.

Neyle tottered over to a far corner of the room and snatched a jar of jellybeans from a shelf. He moved to our circle and chose a spot between Abbey and Baker. After handing the jar to Abbey, he unfolded his seat. He grunted as he straddled the makeshift chair and let his hands rest on the curved top of the cane. He waited as Luther powered down his machine, smiled as Sing checked her watch for the thirtieth time, arched his eyebrows as Baker picked his nose, and furrowed his brow at the way Abbey grimaced over the candy jar like someone had asked to her hold dirty underwear.

He never made eye contact with me.

"I'll take those back, Abbey dear. Alright, y'all know the drill."

I considered raising my hand to inform him I had no clue what the *drill* was — and that I was alive and not a ghost in the room. But he continued before I got the chance.

"Progress report, I'll start. The good: My physical therapist says I'm making real strides. The bad: I still can't write with a pen, and my darn right foot doesn't always do what my left-brain tells it. Laura says she can sympathize with my left-brain, because I don't always do what she tells me, either."

He chuckled and grabbed a handful of jellybeans before passing the jar to Baker. Neyle had a slight droop to his mouth that was hard to see under the bushy mustache. Stroke maybe?

Baker tossed back several beans. "Good: Totally made it to all my classes but two last week." There was a chorus of surprised murmurs. "Bad: I only remember going to Algebra, man."

Groans rained down. Baker shrugged and snatched another handful of candy. He shoved the jar into my hands. I immediately attempted to hand them over to Luther, but he simply regarded me with wide-eyed incredulity—like I'd used the Holy Water at a Catholic mass to wash my armpits or something.

I watched Neyle. My gut tightened. Did he expect me to participate in confessional on my first night?

He smiled.

"I really don't know why I'm here—"

Neyle held his hand up. "Maybe start with your name."

"Right," I mumbled. "My name is Ernie. I'm a sophomore. I play ... I played baseball here at South State."

I tried to pass the candy off once more. Luther shook his head, so I grabbed a few out of the jar and tried again. He still wouldn't take the damn thing.

Neyle coughed. "Nice to meet you, Ernie. How about your week? Anything good or bad to report?"

"For real?" I hoped to find some kind of support but only got a toothy grin from Abbey and a frustrated eye roll from Sing for my effort.

"Okay, guess I'll go bad first since there's been a lot to choose from lately. I managed to royally piss off my new English teacher. Good..." I scratched at my chin, which was beginning to stubble over for the night. Surely I'd had something worthwhile happen. "They had corn chip chili pies in the cafeteria on Monday?"

"Those are awesome, bro." Baker leaned forward. "You put that nacho cheese on them?"

Abbey made a dramatic gagging sound. In spite of my annoyed mood, I couldn't hold back a smile.

I popped a jellybean into my mouth, then handed the jar to Luther and was almost giddy when he took it. I thought I caught the hint of a wink from Neyle.

He relaxed on his seat. "Lex, what was up with you?"

"Bad: Dad is still an asshole. Good: I didn't actually have to talk to him this week. Next."

Luther placed the jar near Sing and fished out a handful of candy.

"Whoa, hold up." Neyle leaned forward. "You didn't have your mid-week check in with the Sergeant?"

Luther shook his head, making his glasses wobble. "Nah, he and Mom went to Vegas to meet up with some of his Army buddies."

"That's progress at least. You must feel like a free man," Neyle said and laughed.

"Not really. He had Mom inform me that re-charging my meal card would have to wait until he got back, so he could go over my purchases from last month. Apparently, I went a little heavy on the snack bar. Guess he's decided to starve me out for insubordination."

"No way," Baker said.

Sing flinched.

Abbey quit fiddling with her nails.

Would his dad really let him go hungry to teach him a lesson?

Not for the first time in my life, I reminded myself that not having a dad around could actually be a bonus. Especially if he was a shitty dad.

"Do you have enough money to eat until then?" Neyle asked.

"Yeah, I'm cool. I've got rations stashed in my dorm for such an emergency. Plus, Mom'll send me some cash if she can sneak out to a mailbox."

Neyle's gaze stayed locked on Luther. "Sing?"

She had arranged six jellybeans into two symmetrical rows in front of her on a piece of seamlessly folded tissue paper. Each candy was a different color — white, green, yellow, black, red, and blue. Judging by how she composed the room earlier before sitting down, she seemed like a girl who had a reason for the order in which she did everything. I couldn't fathom the meaning of this, though.

"Good: I stopped by the housing office and asked for a roommate request form."

Neyle grinned. "That's great, Sing. We've talked about you getting a roomy for a couple of semesters now. You know, Laura and I probably wouldn't be married if it weren't for Hyena Brown, my old college roommate. He'd eat anything, and we often *had* to because we were so poor. If I could survive a year with Hyena, I knew Laura's cooking wouldn't kill me, either. Don't tell her I said that. "

Sing smiled.

"Bet you didn't even take an application, did you?" Luther asked.

Sing turned on him, teeth bared like a prim-but-very-wild, animal.

"Of course I didn't. The student secretary bimbo behind the desk was eating cheesy chips and put her gross hands all over it. I asked for an application, not a passport to her personal island of disease and filth."

Luther laughed.

Neyle crossed his arms over his chest. "You didn't say that to her, did you?"

Sing fiddled with her candy, not making eye contact with anyone. "That's actually my bad thing for the week. They threatened to call campus security if I didn't leave. So I told them I'd gladly go with security—or anyone—with table manners beyond that of the common house rat."

Neyle sighed. "Well, I can print one up for you I suppose. That leaves you, Abbey."

She sifted through the candy jar and selected a single, pink bean. She took a tiny nibble and set the other half of the piece on the floor in front of her with a satisfied, and gorgeous, smile.

"Give me a break." Luther moaned.

She narrowed her eyes. "It's called portion control."

"It's called neurosis, aka why we're freaking here," Luther replied.

If a look could gouge eyes out, Luther would've been left with an extra set of nostrils in his head. Abbey's fury didn't last long, however.

"Good: Becca wanted me to go on this new diet with her, where you eat nothing but green juices for a month." She stuck her chest out and smoothed her hair. "I said no."

"Doesn't take a genius to know you can't survive off liquids," Luther said. "I'm not sure that's a win."

"Not true, bro," Baker said, his voice taking on the quality of a wise surfer guru. "I once bet my brother's friend he couldn't survive a month living on those diet meal replacement shakes. Gained like twenty-five pounds."

"Your bad thing?" Neyle asked. An edge of impatience in his voice told me he was trying desperately to usher us beyond the introductory round at this point.

"So, I was at the mall last weekend, and I tried on this ultra-cute top. It had this *amazing* scalloped lace on the sleeves and a deep neckline. Which I totally adore, because I think my collarbones are my best feature and—"

Neyle cleared his throat, again.

Abbey's eyes widened. "Anyway, they only had an extra-small in the mint color I liked. I tried it on and it made my arms look all bulgy. I mean totally like cookie dough covered in plastic wrap. But I bought it anyway."

"You got the shirt even though you didn't look good in it?" Sing asked. "Sounds like a good thing coming from University Barbie."

Had to admit, I was slightly impressed this girl got something that she felt was less than flattering on her.

Abbey stared at the ceiling and crossed her lean arms. "I figured I could squeeze into it if I made good food choices during the week. So I decided to skip food on Tuesday and Thursday. The top is really cute, though…"

The silence got uncomfortable, quick, and I felt bad for her.

"You skipped a meal on a couple of days. Seems okay to me," I said.

I scanned the group, not understanding why no one was backing me up. She didn't need to beat herself up over what I was sure every girl did on occasion. When Neyle retrieved a packet of travel tissues from his shirt pocket as a tear worked its way down Abbey's cheek, I knew.

I'd misunderstood. She literally didn't eat anything two full days because she thought a shirt looked funny on her. The true burden of what we were doing settled over me in that moment. These weren't quirky people. These were sick people. They needed medicine—be it a figurative ointment for the soul or a very real pill for the body—or their disease was going to kill them. And I was one of them.

Chapter Eight

After I'd successfully stuck my entire leg in my mouth like a pro jackass, group counseling had continued for nearly a full hour of crying, yelling, silence, and laughter. I was tapped out emotionally, and my head ached as if someone had tried to land a cargo jet between my ears. One thing I knew: catharsis was a hell of a lot of work.

I hoped I'd eventually feel good after these gatherings, because right then, I felt like I'd been put through a psychological washing machine on the heavy-duty cycle.

There had been some positives, however. Taking part in the group was like seeing my own distorted reflection in water. We were different on the outside, but ultimately made up of the same substance. All of us were really good at some things, but really crappy at others.

Sing camped on the Dean's honor role but couldn't get along with others to the point she'd been dropped from classes for arguing with the professors. Baker played five instruments and was in three different bands at any given time, but he liked weed so much, he couldn't make it to two classes a week. On the other hand, Luther was super-focused but was so afraid of disappointing his father, he wouldn't drop his pre-med degree track and chase his dream of creating video games. Abbey was gorgeous and loved by pretty much everyone, but she hated herself so much she couldn't see it.

After only one session, I realized this might be the team I belonged on most. Which offered a soothing balm on my otherwise raw psyche.

Luther and I strolled quietly across campus. Our dorms were in the same general direction, so we'd decided to walk together.

"That was way heavier than I expected," I said.

"Yeah." Luther never took his attention away from messing with his phone. "I always hate going, but I'm always glad I went. Sort of like my grandma's house as a kid."

I laughed. "What are you doing for your homework assignment again?"

At the close of the session, Neyle issued the proclamation that we were to each pick a task of personal growth to complete before our next meeting.

"Figure I'll tell Dad how shitty it was to withhold food money just because I didn't do what he wanted."

"And how do you think that'll go?"

Luther chuckled humorlessly. "I'll make sure to tell him in a public place so he doesn't kick my ass. What about you? You said you're going to apologize to someone. Have you identified a target?"

This guy was *really* into his military video games.

I stared up at the stars and counted at least a dozen in my head. "I've got someone in mind."

We reached the place where our paths split—right to the athletic dorms, left to the regular dorms.

Luther turned to me. "Cool meeting you."

"Same."

I stuck my hand out and he shook it, revealing a jagged stretch of scar on his wrist.

He twisted his arm to hide the swollen, pink flesh. "I was in a pretty bad place a year ago."

I sighed. "I've been thinking of going to that *place* myself. That's how I ended up at tonight's party, in fact."

Luther nodded knowingly. "You made the right choice. I should've gotten help sooner. Catch you at the next meeting?"

"Sure." He made to walk away, but I touched his shoulder to stop him. "Here, let me give you my number. If you get hungry, text me. I'm still on scholarship until the end of the semester. My meal plan never runneth dry."

Luther smiled and entered my number into his phone. "Thanks, man."

The next morning, I stood in front of the partially cracked office door. The target of my homework assignment was inside. I could hear her typing like mad with an occasional "shit" thrown in, probably when she'd screw something up. My gut churned uncomfortably, and I was fairly sure the iced coffee I'd snagged from the campus corner store on the way over wasn't the source of my indigestion.

This wouldn't be the easiest way to experience *personal growth*. I didn't always have a lot to say in general, especially to people who despised me for being me. Furthermore, "sorry" wasn't exactly ready to dive off of the tip of my tongue in this scenario. I'd barely gotten a complete sentence out the last time we'd talked without her diving down my throat.

Still, Ms. Price, the graduate assistant turned professor, had stirred something in me. After talking to her, I'd felt annoyed and angry, sure. Maybe even a little turned on. But I'd *felt*. For some inexplicable reason, I cared what she thought about me, at a point in my life when I scarcely gave a shit about what I thought about myself.

Ultimately, I would have to have a conversation with Junkyard that would also involve the S word. That discussion wasn't likely to be as pleasant as this one, so I considered this good practice with someone who wasn't going to break my nose if I screwed it up. She could certainly fail me, but I wasn't sure my college career would go beyond this semester anyway.

I rapped on the door.

There was a flurry of movement before, "Come in."

I wiped my moist hands on my jeans and grabbed the doorknob.

Margery wore an oversized crimson and gold university hoody. A red ponytail dangled from the back of her baseball cap.

"Oh, I … Office hours aren't until this afternoon. Agnes at the front desk should've—"

"She wasn't there. I'll be quick."

She tugged at the sleeves of her sweatshirt and straightened her glasses. "It's Ernest, right?"

"Call me Ernie."

"Very good." She inclined her head. "Have a seat, Ernie."

I slumped into one of the tiny office chairs. "I'm sorry to bother you. I wanted to talk to you about class the other day. And I want to officially apologize for what I called you in the library."

Her eyebrows arched. A shallow porcelain mug with a tea tag hanging over the lip sat to her left. *Oh bugger!* was written on the side in scrawling cursive. She took a sip. "That really isn't necessary."

"No, it is." I leaned forward. "I have to."

"What do you mean *have to*? You know, a forced apology isn't really an apology. Unless you're five years old."

I sighed. *My God, did she make everything this impossible?*

"It's not forced. I got to pick who I apologized to."

"Lucky me." The corner of her mouth twitched up with the shadow of a grin. "Might I ask who sent you on this quest for redemption?"

"I'm in counseling."

She shifted in her seat. I got a strong impression that if she'd had a panic button under her desk, she might have pressed it.

I massaged my temples. "That came out wrong. I'm not nuts—well, I might be. It's something I'm working on."

She took another sip of tea. "That's … good."

"When you bumped into me at the library, I'd been having a run of epically bad days. Looking back on it, I see that you were probably nervous for your first teaching day."

Her cup clanked when she placed it back on the desk. "I wasn't nervous."

I smiled. "Trust me, I can spot big game jitters. You seemed a little on edge."

"You startled me." Her cheeks reddened to a color a shade lighter than her hair.

"I was talking about after class."

"Oh … well, I meant what I said. Athletes won't get a free ride from me." Her tone wasn't threatening, just resolute. *Progress.*

"And I'm not asking for one."

"Fair enough. What else can I do for you?"

She lifted the cup to her mouth again. The way the subtle texture of her lips creased along the smooth glass sent a small excited shiver down my spine. I relaxed back into my seat and picked at one of the frayed holes in my jeans to distract me from my *other* thoughts.

"I'm not who you think I am you know," I said at last.

"I know."

I looked up at her.

"You do?"

She gave me an apologetic smile, pursing a couple of slight dimples in her cheeks.

She'd been more right than she knew, comparing me to a little boy earlier. Like a smitten fifth grader, I had a full-on, mind-numbing crush on my new teacher. And it was the third strike on any worthwhile apology I could have ever come up with. But I realized I wasn't here to make amends at all. I'd come here to see Margery again.

"I did some research on you after class." She opened a drawer and withdrew a folder. My name was on the tab at the top. "There have been three papers assigned so far in your class. I've graded two of those. Yours have been the best I've read, by a large margin. You're insightful, articulate, and you draw bold conclusions. I'd take twenty more of you in a heartbeat."

My cheeks warmed, and hers reddened once more.

"Thanks. I hope that means you'll give me a another chance."

She removed her glasses and rubbed the bridge of her nose. "Ernie, you have to understand where I come from. My dad is a big personality on this campus, as I'm sure you know."

I raised my eyebrows, truly not sure what she was talking about.

"Oh God." It was her turn to massage her head. "You don't know, do you?"

"No clue. But call me intrigued."

"Your baseball coach is my father."

My jaw was hanging open, but words weren't coming out. The air had quit moving from my lungs as well. Did I have a sign on my back that read "life craps here" or something?

"That sounded very Darth Vader-ish, didn't it?""How

… but … shit … I mean, wow! Sorry?"

She laughed. "It's okay. My entire existence has been dominated by baseball. It's how I spent all of my summers growing up. I ate dinner on team busses, learned to ride a bike in parking lots behind stadiums, celebrated most of my birthdays in the bleachers — it was all baseball, all the time. I suppose I owe him credit for turning me on to literature at least. Reading was about the only way I kept my sanity. He named me after the former chain-smoking owner of the Cincinnati Reds for Heaven's sake."

I shook my head with a sudden realization. *Of course…*

"I'd hate me too if I were in your position," I said.

"I don't hate *you*. I hate baseball — or what it signifies in my life at least."

I grinned. "That's good, because I don't play anymore."

Her brow furrowed, her mouth taking a skeptical, upward turn. "You don't?"

"It's a long story. I kind of — "

A phone on the desk chirped. Margery snatched it up.

"Damnit. I'm late." She put her hand over her mouth and glanced up at me. "I'm so sorry. Baseball players literally taught me my first words. Picked up a bit of a potty mouth as a result."

I stood. "I've heard it before. Trust me. Thanks for your time."

"You're welcome. Stop by anytime."

"I just might."

I paused at the door and turned to face her. Our eyes

met. She started messing with her phone again, but she'd been staring at me. I was sure of it.

"Apology accepted?"

"Wha—what?" she asked, looking more disheveled than perplexed.

"The apology. Accepted?"

She pursed her lips. "This is really important to you, isn't it?"

"Yes."

As she shoed me from the room, she smiled. "Yes, apology accepted. I'll see you in class."

After the door clicked shut, I leaned against the wall and laughed. Margery was beautiful, smart, and she thought I was gifted at something other than baseball. She also happened to be the daughter of the person who hated me most in the world, but her relationship with him didn't seem much better than mine. *The perfect girl.*

Chapter Nine

Luther slurped his soda and stuffed three more fries into his mouth. He wore a shirt with a bull's-eye on it that read *I fragged your mom.*

"You like her," he said in between smacks.

I'd told him about my successful apology to Margery.

"No." I pulled my sweatshirt hood over my head, hoping he wouldn't see me grinning like an idiot. "She's cool ... and gorgeous ... and smart, I'll grant you. But she hates baseball, and maybe me by association, so we're clearly not a match."

"Glad you think so, because she's your teacher and a graduate student. She'd get fired and probably expelled for screwing around with a student."

I tried not to flinch, but if Luther could have seen my heart, I was sure he'd have noticed a lapse between beats. The whole teacher-student thing hadn't darkened my mind.

Not that any rational part of me was actually considering parleying our somewhat antagonistic relationship into something more. But the fifth grade boy in me was still undoubtedly infatuated with her. Whatever silly fantasies I'd briefly entertained — like running my callused pitching fingers over the smooth skin of her stomach or being close enough to her to smell the shampoo in her hair — were extinguished by Luther's Good Dream Bucket Brigade. *Damn him.*

"Of course. I knew that." I stabbed the husk of my baked potato repeatedly with my plastic knife. "She's in grad school and I'm a sophomore, so she's probably three or four years older than me anyway. You think she likes younger guys?"

Luther eyed me like I'd been stuffed so full of shit, it was running out of my ears. "You're ridiculous."

"And you're dumb." I chucked the knife at him.

He threw a fry back at me and laughed. I batted it down and smiled.

"What are you two fruit flies doing?" Junkyard strolled toward us, a small burger in each of his bulky hands. I pushed a chair away from the table, which he straddled with a growl.

"Sup?" I pointed across the table. "This is Luther."

"Hey," Luther said, looking more impressed than shocked when Junk shoved an entire burger into his mouth.

Junkyard nodded and grabbed my drink. He swigged half of it down and belched. "What're you up to tonight?"

I shrugged. "Same old. Study a little, probably — "

Junkyard smacked his knee. "You're a real riot. It's Friday, loser. Darko is having people over. His uncle owns an inflatable games businesses, and we've got the boxing ring and giant gloves for the whole weekend. I'm going to hammer on that bitch Goldstein until he cries or agrees to give me his Web porn passwords."

Junk crammed down his other burger. He put his trash on my tray, of course, and pointed at me. "Trashcan punch, babes, and games. You're coming. Bring Deadeye here with you if you want."

"He was ... interesting," Luther said as we left the cafeteria.

"I've known Junkyard most of my life. He's rough on the outside, but he's a decent guy down deep. Okay, sometimes you have to mine for the good guy tendencies. Guess we're more like brothers at this point. You coming with me tonight or what?"

Luther gave me a skeptical glance. "I'm seriously invited?"

"You heard Junk. Have to tell you, he doesn't extend invitations by accident."

He beamed. "I don't know, I'd have to re-schedule our clan practice and—"

I put my arm around him. "I'm going to introduce you to the seedy world of underground inflatable game boxing. It's like an anti-fight club for morons, and someone will probably pee their pants laughing ... or because they're drunk. And talking about it afterwards, especially if there are embarrassing pics you can post online, is highly encouraged."

The scene at Darko's was an appropriately eclectic college affair. Groups of all sizes and types mingled in pockets on the front lawn and inside the home. Music thumped from somewhere out back, so we headed there.

Twinkling Christmas lights were strung from the eaves of the house to the fence surrounding the backyard. A pair of woolly trees hunkered in one corner, and a giant inflatable ring loomed in the other.

Two girls rolled around with their oversized boxing gloves on, laughing more than fighting. Darko refereed the bout. He wore his ever-present mirrored sunglasses and a striped official's shirt with the sleeves ripped off. A red plastic cup sloshed in one hand and a whistle twirled in the other. People—mostly dudes—had gathered to watch the ladies tangle. Occasionally someone would encourage one of them to pull the other's top off. They were already in their bras, so I thought it might actually happen if things continued down the current dubious course.

I looked over my shoulder for Luther. He stood about five feet behind me, watching the girls grapple. I tugged his arm. "Want something to drink?"

Luther blinked dazedly. "Sure."

We made our way to the giant black trashcan, strategically stationed in the middle of the yard. I plucked a soda from a nearby ice chest. Luther eyed the red brew of punch and floating fruit.

"Want some?" I asked.

"I'm not twenty-one."

I grabbed a cup and fished some out for him. "I'm guessing you aren't the only one. I'll make sure you get home."

He took a sip with a curious but satisfied smile. His nose crinkled.

"Don't like it?"

"You kidding? It's amazing! What's in it?"

"Probably everything Darko had left over from his last party." I laughed. "Be careful. It sneaks up on you."

"Roger that." Luther offered me a mock salute with his cup hand. "You don't drink?"

"Not much. I tend to spend a lot of miserable time in my own head as it is. Alcohol makes it worse. And Mom said my old man had a thing for cheap whiskey. Made him mean according to her, so I figure why chance it."

We found Junkyard and Bash watching the girls fight. Judging by the pink mustache Junk had grown, he'd been enjoying the punch, too.

Bash put his arm around my neck. "Just in time for the show, buddy."

"Why is your shirt unbuttoned? Are those gold chains?" I swiped at Bash's hairless chest and he ducked away.

"Chicks dig it," Bash said, adjusting his pants so a healthy amount of boxer short peeked out the top.

"I bet." I turned to Junk. "What's the good word?"

"They've still got their clothes on." He punched me on the arm. "This is bullshit."

"There's no justice," I said and smiled. "You remember Luther?"

He hugged Luther, making his eyes bulge as he squeezed. "Welcome to fight night. How do you know my boy?"

"We bumped into each other." Luther took a nervous sip of punch. "On campus the other day."

Junk narrowed his eyes. "You met at the shrink?"

I nodded and swallowed an uncomfortable lump in my throat. I had no clue where Junk would take this, seeing as he didn't think my head needed much straightening to begin with.

"That's cool," Junkyard said his tone thoughtful and quiet. He took a drink of his punch.

"You guys got any extra cash?" Bash poked his head between us. "I'm trying to get some bets going."

Luther shook his head, but I fished a five out of my pocket and handed the money over. Junkyard and Bash disappeared, leaving Luther and me in silence. The girls had finished. Now, four skinny guys were going at it tag team style.

"Your buddy okay with you being in counseling?" Luther asked.

"Not sure."

I truly wasn't sure what it meant between Junk and me. Alone, I didn't think he gave a damn one way or the other. But if I ever told him the truth about the game, would he see me going to counseling as an excuse? In his eyes, I could understand how it might look like I'd opted to blame my past troubles for my present problems instead of owning up to my mistake. Hell, that was how I felt half the time, which was why the need to confess to him had been weighing on me so much. Somehow, I had to make him understand that the festering wound I'd been walking around with most of my life had finally gone septic and left me crippled.

The tag team match ended abruptly when one of the competitors accidentally bloodied his opponent's nose. The onlookers drifted away. Darko hurried onto the matt to make an announcement.

"Ladies and miscreants, gather round for the main event."

"This should be good," I whispered to Luther. "Wonder who the idiots are?"

"In this corner," Darko shouted, "we've got The Beast of the South State Wild—and your star catcher. Behold, the Junkyard Dog."

Junk bounced to center ring, wearing nothing but his boxer-briefs, a pair of blue inflatable boxing gloves, a carpet's worth of hair on his barrel chest, and a gap-toothed smile. There were catcalls from some girls standing near us—a few from guys as well. Junk gave the latter a crossed-arm FU.

"Who in the hell did they convince to fight him?" I asked, already feeling sorry for the poor bastard. "Please tell me it's not Bash. Junk can literally bench press two of him."

I'd wrestled Junk plenty of times, goofing around. It was like fighting a sweaty boulder with a yellow Mohawk.

"I don't know." Luther downed the rest of his cocktail in a single gulp. "But if he's not wearing pants either, I'm going to need another drink."

Luther wandered away.

Darko scanned the crowd, which was growing exponentially.

"Where is he? There." He pointed in my general direction. I took a cautious step backward.

"Hawk, get up here and face your doom."

I held my hands up and smiled. "I don't think so."

Junk pointed at me with one arm and flexed his other. "Ernie, get your ass up here or I'll drag you up by your ball hairs. These people want a show."

Darko hopped off the ring and jogged over to me.

"That's right, folks. We've got pitcher versus catcher — best friends battling to the bitter end. Place your bets."

"I'm not doing this, Darko." I removed his arm from around my shoulders.

Junk and I needed to talk, not fake fight. On top of that, he'd been oddly contemplative since I'd been kicked off of the team. Something was eating him, and I guessed what it was. He wasn't convinced I'd simply screwed up. We'd been too good of friends for too long for him not to sense that. Junk was also horrible at articulating anything remotely close to a feeling. Putting the pieces together, I figured this might be his attempt at working through this. Combined with booze and crowd of onlookers, I couldn't think of a worse way for him to navigate his issues with me.

Bash came up behind me. He leaned in close enough to whisper in my ear. "C'mon, Ernie. People are already placing bets. I know Junk's going to kick your ass, and you know it. But the freshman don't. I'm going to clean up. Do it for a friend."

Darko grinned. "We're talking an entire semester of my parties funded, Ernie. That's like getting free admission to an adult's only theme park."

I scanned the crowd. There were a *lot* of eyes staring at me. A lot of them were very pretty female eyes. It might do my self-image some good to be something other than the guy who lost the big game. My chest swelled. Wherever the macho switch inside my body was located, Darko had found and flicked it. *Fuck.*

"You get five minutes." I let him guide me to the ring. "Five minutes."

"Right, right," Darko said patting the plastic, bouncy platform. "Shoes off. And you might want to ditch the rest, too."

He'd already shoved me onto the mat before I could protest. Junk bounced from foot-to-foot like an uncoordinated Mohammad Ali. The jostling of the bouncy inflatable surface made getting to my feet a chore.

"Why do I need to be in my underwear?" I shouted to Darko, who ignored me.

I checked out Junk, who simply smiled and nodded. "No. I'm not taking my pants off. No."

"And, in a special one-night-only event," Darko said. "This will be our first ever lukewarm oil match."

A plastic jug of vegetable oil was tossed up to Darko, who immediately unscrewed the lid and dumped the thick, golden contents into the center of the ring. He hopped over to me.

"Like I said, might want to shuck some clothes."

I glared at him. "I'm going to kill you for this."

He waved the empty jug and laughed. "My uncle is going to do it for you. But I'm too drunk to care. Touch gloves and fight."

He rolled off the ring.

"I don't have gloves," I said, shimmying out of my jeans.

I only had two pair of pants with no holes in them, and I sure as hell wasn't going to destroy one of them oil wrestling with Junk. Thank God I'd done my laundry and actually had clean boxers to wear instead of going commando as I'd been known to do on occasion.

Before I could get my shirt all the way over my head, I was slammed to the spongy surface. Junk laughed hysterically from somewhere on top of me, as he pummeled me with the soft, plastic gloves. The crowd erupted with cheers.

Luckily, he was so covered in oil already, it was pretty easy to squirm out of his grasp. Unluckily, I still had my socks on, so I looked ridiculous in front of a few dozen of my peers and sundry hot girls.

"If this ends up on the campus website, I'll burn your future homes to the ground," I said to no one in particular.

I spied the other set of gloves and put them on while Junk struggled to get to his feet. He barreled toward me but slipped into a slide. I tried to hop over him, but he caught my legs, and we both ended up on the mat in a tangle. I used my legs to scissor his chest and hold him in place, then I beat him about the head with my free glove.

Eventually, we slipped away from each other, but I

could hardly stay on my feet as the oil had covered every inch of everything. I couldn't stop laughing. We danced a few feet away from each other, trying to act like real boxers, and then moved in to grapple again.

"Fun, right?" Junk yelled into my ear, as we exchanged blows and hugs.

"It kind of is." I tripped him. "But I still hate your ass for this."

I popped him in the forehead a couple of times before he finally used his added weight to get leverage and flip me onto my back. We struggled, and one of my gloves must have fallen off. Before I realized what happened, I whacked him in the face with my bare fist.

We went completely still. My fist stung from the blow, so I knew the hit had to have hurt. Junk pawed at his nose to check for blood. I saw a familiar malice rising in his eyes. He'd nearly killed me the one and only time I'd hit him with a pitch in practice.

"You alright?" I asked. "Maybe we should call—"

"Like hell," he said and put me in headlock. "It ends when you yield."

He came at me like some kind of pissed off gladiator. I fought with his arms to no use. He was too strong.

"Seriously?" I asked. "You're going to make me give up?"

"That's right." He loosened his grip some, and leaned in close to my ear. "Or you can tell me the truth about what happened at the game."

The odor of alcohol on his breath was palpable. I went

stiff. My instincts had told me that was what this was truly about. He was frustrated and confused, so naturally, thrashing me in front of people would resolve all of our problems. *What an ass.*

My face warmed, more from anger than the pooling of blood from Junk's chokehold. "We can talk about that somewhere else…"

He strengthened his hold enough to make getting a good breath a chore. "Bullshit. This is as good a place as any."

The onlookers yelled as Darko tried to secure some last-second wagers, so I didn't think we'd drawn much attention yet.

"You don't want to hear that. Not now. You're drunk."

He squeezed tighter, and I struggled harder, digging my fingers into his biceps. Blood thundered in my ears as my airway got smaller.

"So what if I *am* drunk? I'm your best friend. You owe me the truth. I've heard what other people think. Now you tell me. Did you hit that batter on purpose?"

I couldn't get enough air in to speak, so I grabbed at his head. Little black dots floated in my vision.

"We have our winner." Darko slid into place beside us. He forced his arms between us. "C'mon, guys. Cut it out. This is supposed to be fun, assholes."

Something must have clicked in Junk, because he let go. I pushed away from him, gasping for air. My eyes watered. The entire world had a fog over it, like I'd been doing shots for the last half hour and horsing around with a *friend.*

Junk tried to shake my hand. I shoved it away.

"Ernie, I'm sorry... I said I'm sorry, man," Junk yelled.

My shirt had gotten flung into the ring, so I picked it up before hopping off. Bash greeted me, putting his hand on my shoulder. I shrugged it off and snatched up my pants and shoes.

I spun on Junkyard. "No, goddamnit. I'm sorry. Okay? It's me who is sorry. I did it on purpose and I'm a fucking sorry person. Find a better best friend."

I shoved by the crowd who was only shimmering apparitions through a prism of my tears.

Chapter Ten

I stood in front of my motorcycle, cursing the stars. My keys must have fallen out of my pocket during GWS the fight. Not that I would have left without Luther, but I'd planned on circling the block until I saw him come out. Adding to the humiliation, I was shirtless because I'd dropped mine in the dirt on the way out. The fabric was so soaked with vegetable oil, it had turned to mud on impact.

Now I got to sit outside of a giant party, where I'd made a complete ass of myself, because I was too ashamed to go back in and find my keys. *Oh what a fucking night.*

"You okay?" a female voice asked from behind me.

I laughed, a hysterical and stupid sound. "Nope. I'm actually the opposite of okay. If *okay* is north, I'm south. If *okay* was a cellular signal, I'd have no damn bars. I'm spectacularly, unerringly not okay. Thanks for asking."

"Alright," she said. "Don't get snippy."

There was something in her voice, an agitated quality I

recognized. I twisted and saw a ponytail of red hair swishing away from me.

"Ms. Price?"

She froze, almost like she hoped if she stood still long enough, I might forget she'd ever spoken to me. The joke was on her. I didn't think I could ever forget a single thing she did.

She turned to face me wearing a smirk. "It's Margery out here in the wild. You spend every Friday night oil wrestling in your underwear and getting into embarrassing public arguments with your friends?"

I ran my hand over my hair and grimaced at the oily mess left behind on my skin.

"This is new. At least the arguing part."

She laughed. Some of the stiffness in my neck lessened, and I laughed, too.

"Speaking of how I spend my Friday nights, care to elaborate on why my teacher is out here mixing it up with the commoners?" I asked, putting my hands in my pockets and walking in her direction.

"My friend's boyfriend begged her to come, and guess who got talked into joining? I'm such a sucker for peer pressure. *Don't be such a prude, Margie. You won't see anyone from your classes, Margie,*" she said in a whiny, mocking tone. "And now here you are. With no shirt on."

I chuckled again and, feeling a touch insecure, crossed my arms over my chest.

"Anyway, I was leaving and saw you come out. Thought you might need someone to talk to. I'd offer you a ride home, but I'm walking. That punch has a real kick to it."

"I appreciate the pun, and the offer. But I have to wait on my friend."

"This the same friend in smiley-face bikini briefs who tried to choke you to death a few minutes ago?"

"No, not that one. This one doesn't want to kill me. Not yet at least."

"I'm glad to hear that."

She giggled softly, scuffing her sneakers together in the dirt. Her gaze drifted up to meet mine. Her eyes were flickering shades of green in the moonlight, making me think of tall, cool summer grass begging to be settled down in for long naps.

"You're an odd one, Mr. Demps."

She was using my last name now.

A good thing?

"So I'm told. Usually not that politely, though."

She snorted and stumbled. I grabbed her arm to steady her, before I registered what I was doing. Her hand grasped my bare bicep for support, setting off an excited tingling in my brain. My legs got a touch wobbly when she didn't immediately let go, making me wonder who was supporting whom.

"Sorry, I should probably get going. That punch is really something." She took a couple of uncertain steps away from me.

Shit. Where the hell was Luther? I couldn't let her walk home alone this tipsy. And it wasn't *just* my loins talking. We were off-campus, with no security, in a less-than desirable neighborhood. There were plenty of creeps around. I played ball with half of them.

"How far away from here do you live?" I scanned the house again for signs of Luther.

She shoved her hands into the pockets of her purple corduroy blazer. "A few blocks." She nodded over her shoulder.

"Mind if I keep you company? Think I'll take you up on the talking part."

She pointed at me. "Thought you were waiting on a friend?"

"I'll come back for him."

"Let's stroll." She stumbled again.

"Whoa there. Let's make sure you don't end up with a turned ankle."

I trotted to her side and draped my arm around her shoulders to straighten her.

"Thanks." She wrapped her arm around my torso, and we set off. We'd gone about a half-block when she said, "You've got a lot of muscles."

She squeezed my side, tickling me.

I smiled. "I'm pretty skinny. But baseball keeps me in decent shape. Well, kept me in shape."

Margery looked up at me as we strolled. I was at least a head taller than her, so I guessed her to be around five-foot eight in shoes.

"Tell me."

God help me, she was even more direct drunk. And I'd have poured my soul into a cup and given it to her for safekeeping if she'd asked. Especially when her perfectly full lips were inches from mine.

"I screw things up, sometimes on purpose. We made it to the doorstep of the championship and I yanked the mat out from under us. And I might have some mommy issues."

"Well, that certainly sounds very serious, Mr. Demps." She grinned, but then her face sagged with sadness or concern. "Can't believe my dad didn't have you strung up for that."

"I'm sure he wanted to. He didn't tell you about it?"

Her forehead creased. "We don't talk much. And never about baseball — or Mom."

"Sorry. How long has she been gone?"

Margery laughed, a booming and beautiful noise that echoed in the halo of trees draping over the street above. "She's not dead, just divorced. Happily, I might add."

"And the Walrus is divorced unhappily, I take it?"

"Correct. Wait..." She spun me around to face her. "You call him the Walrus? That's perfect."

"It's the jowls." I pulled my cheeks down with my hands.

We shared another laugh and continued our stroll, but no longer touching. The memory of her warmth lingered pleasantly in my mind.

"What about your folks?" she asked.

I momentarily rethought my stance on telling her everything, and then decided she was likely too drunk to remember anyway.

"Mom died when I was seventeen. Dad went to prison when I was eight. Haven't seen him since. Don't want to."

She whistled. "You win the sucky life grand prize alright. Grandparents? Aunts and uncles? Siblings?"

"Grandfolks are all gone. Only aunts and uncles are on Dad's side, and they hate my guts. Only kid."

"You, Mr. Demps, have to be one lonely young man."

I didn't want to let her know how much those words really scratched me, but there was an undeniable truth in them.

"I'm so sorry."

I must've stiffened or gone quiet. "Not a big deal."

"That wasn't a nice thing to say and—"

I waved dismissively. "It's okay, really. But please, call me Ernie. Mr. Demps makes me sound like one of my dead grandparents. Although, Ernie is definitely an old man name, so maybe it fits."

"Deal." She hooked her arm around mine. "My house is at the end of the street. How *did* you get a name like Ernie?"

"Dad was a big Cubs fan. Ernie Banks was his favorite player."

"Both of us were named for famous baseball personalities. And both of our names belong in a 1950s phone book. We could've been separated at birth, Mr. Ernie," she said.

"Now I sound like a banker or mob boss." I laughed.

We'd reached a break in the trees, so I stopped to contemplate the sky. "Really, I like to think I was named after

Hemingway."

"Your English teacher approves."

Margery tugged at my arm to get me moving, but I pulled her back. A line from a Walt Whitman poem sprang to mind, and I felt compelled to share it with her.

"Then my realities; What else is so real as mine?"

She stared at me, her eyes gleaming above a bemused smile. "You memorize a lot of poetry?"

I nodded. "Mom loved poetry. After she died, I had the hardest time focusing on the field. So I took to memorizing poems and reciting them in my head. Really helped me block out my thoughts."

"Reminds you of her, too, I bet."

"So my psychiatrist tells me." I smiled. "They also usually mean something. Not sure about that one, though. I guess I haven't felt very *real* lately. Tonight is the most grounded I've been in a long time."

We walked up the sidewalk and paused at the steps leading to her front door. The house was small and homey, a perfect little cottage with flowerboxes below the windows and a porch swing.

Margery squeezed and let go of my arm. "Ever think you maybe just need a little help? That it's time to quit trying to do things by yourself? You're a pitcher. If things aren't working, time for a change up."

She tried to take the first step up to the porch, missed, and stumbled backward. I wrapped my arms around her to keep us from falling over. Her hair was silky against my chest. It smelled of jasmine and fruit. Margery's gaze flashed upward, her mouth open in surprise.

"Yes, I had considered I might need a little help," I whispered.

I dipped my head. She tilted hers. Her body went limp, allowing me to cradle hers against mine. Our lips touched lightly at first, and then collided like forces of nature. There was a hidden energy underneath, an excitement, like it was the first or last time we'd touch. She moaned —

"Ernie? That you?" a familiar voice said from behind us.

Margery pushed away from me. She took the three steps of the porch in a single leap. I hung my head.

"Yes." My lips still tingled from the kiss and my heart thumped erratically.

Luther stood where the sidewalk and street met, dangling something shiny from his hand.

"Found your keys, man. Someone said they saw you head this direction. You okay?"

The door to Margery's house banged shut behind me. I considered giving Luther the same terse answer I'd given her earlier in the evening. After all, I was still shirtless, I'd still made a fool of myself, Junk was probably still going to kick my ass, and who knew how far out of bounds I'd stepped with Margery. She might never speak to me again once she sobered up.

In spite of all the things that could go wrong, I smiled. "For once, yeah. I think I'm good."

Chapter Eleven

Neyle grimaced as he stretched his leg. He plucked the strings of his ukulele, creating a twinkling jumble of high-pitched tones.

"Since Ernie was the only one to successfully carry out his homework assignment this week, we're going to have a little sing along."

I got a round of hateful looks from everyone but Baker. He was busy running his fingers over the carpet with the awestruck expression of a baby tasting his first ice cream. I waved at the scowling faces.

Was it my fault the target of my homework happened to be a beautiful graduate assistant for whom I'd have set my shoes on fire to get her attention? I didn't think so.

"We'll start with Baker since he knows how the game works," Neyle said, strumming chords in a surprisingly melodic fashion.

He can really play.

"The basic idea is to come up with your own meaningful lyrics to a familiar tune. We'll do Over the Rainbow tonight. Sound good?"

"Does having your eyelids removed *sound good*?" Sing grumbled, adjusting the rubber bands around her pigtails.

Unaffected, Neyle jangled through the opening chords a few times and sang, "Somewhere, over the rainbow..."

He nodded at Baker, continuing to play.

"There's a free pizza pie," Baker said to a chorus of laughter.

"Good," Neyle said. "There's a land..."

"Where the food won't go straight to my thighs," Abbey sang.

"Somewhere, over the rainbow..."

"The people are few," Sing sang.

"And the..."

"High scores in games will apply to real life, too," Luther droned tunelessly.

Oh hell, my turn was next.

"Someday I'll..."

Crap. Crap. Crap. Neyle kept strumming the same chord and smiling at me.

"Wish upon a star and wake up with my degree beside me?"

Neyle nodded excitedly. "Where troubles melt like lemon drops..."

"And *high* above the chimney tops is where'll you find me, bro," Baker said, trying to high five Abbey, who ignored him.

"I bet," Luther replied.

Even Neyle got a chuckle out of that one. After he'd composed himself, we did another round, and then got down to the business of group counseling. When the session ended, we gathered on the front porch of the Fredrick House.

Luther and Baker showed me a video of their most recent gaming conquest they'd uploaded to the Web. Abbey and Sing chatted nearby.

My stomach gurgled. "Anyone else hungry?"

"Food sounds like a win to me," Baker said, already exploring the pockets of his tattered jacket. I assumed he was digging for change.

"You guys ever eat at Big Burrito across from campus?" I asked, still trying to figure out the thought Abbey had spurred in me.

Abbey hopped up and down. "They have a sprouts and veggie bowl that literally makes me lustful."

Luther frowned. "Where I come from, burritos are wrapped in tortillas, not served in bowls. They put things like chicken and salsa inside, not gross, worm-like green stuff."

Abbey stuck her tongue out and he smiled.

"I'm game." Sing stood. "But if any of you use their filthy public restroom, you can't sit at my table."

After building our burritos and bowls in the food line, all of us — minus Sing — crowded onto the benches at a corner table. She pulled up her own chair.

"We haven't done diagnosis roulette since Ernie joined the group. What do you guys think?" Abbey used her napkin to cover her mouth as she spoke.

"Diagnosis roulette? Sounds dangerous," I said.

Luther clapped me on the shoulder. "It is. That's why it's fun."

"Totally, bro. We spin the straw and the two people it points to have to guess each other's diagnosis. " Baker pulled the straw out of his drink and slapped it in the middle of the table.

Sing's eyes bulged. "That's so gross. I'm not touching it."

"You're not playing anyway. Newbie is the only one who doesn't know what's wrong with us. He gets to spin." Luther gestured toward the straw.

It barely went around once and pointed at Abbey.

She grinned. "Go ahead, Ernie. Take a guess."

I chewed on a bite of burrito for a long time. How does one politely point out another person's psychological malady?

"Anorexia," I said, trying not to look at her directly.

Luther snickered. Baker tried to hide a smile with his cup.

"What's so funny?" I asked.

"He's an amateur, guys. Go easy on him," Abbey said, her tone teasing.

My ears warmed. "Okay, what is it then?"

"My official diagnosis is FED-NEC."

"Sounds … complicated. Do you need, like, a permit for it?"

Abbey laughed. "It stands for Feeding or Eating Disorders Not Elsewhere Classified. It's atypical Anorexia Nervosa. I display many of the Anorexia symptoms, but my weight stays pretty well in the normal range. Doctor Jones thinks I might also be in the early stages of Orthorexia."

"Which is?"

"An obsession with healthy eating."

Luther typed frantically on his phone.

I scowled at him. "Are you taking notes?"

"That's one I haven't heard of before." He put his phone away and smiled. "Did we forget to mention that loser buys dinner after our next group session?"

"My turn," Abbey said. "Let's see. You're kind of quiet. A little surly—"

"I'm not surly."

Baker shrugged. "You're kind of surly, bro."

I rolled my eyes. "Whatever."

"See, surly," Sing said.

I laughed. "Hey pot, the kettle said to quit calling names."

Sing raised her eyebrows. "At least I own it."

"Anyway, I'm thinking you're carrying some guilt around—probably thinking about death as viable exit strategy. You did something drastic to dissociate from your regular life, like quitting the baseball team. Which is why you ended up with us. My guess is Major Depressive Disorder."

"Nailed it." Luther reached over the table to high five her.

"Nailed what? I didn't quit the baseball team. They fired me—with cause, granted. And I haven't been given an official diagnosis. I'm meeting with Doctor Laura tomorrow to find out."

I made a mental note to look up Major Depressive Disorder.

"Face it, man." Luther stuck his chest out. "I'm a MDD, and you fit the bill. Abbey never gets it wrong."

"It's true. She's like Rain Man for crazy people syndromes," Sing said, only looking mildly unaffected.

"Fine. I bet I can guess yours, Sing. Obsessive Compulsive Disorder."

She chuckled like I'd tried to kick a soccer ball and missed. "That's one of them, Mr. Holmes. Care to take as stab at the others?"

"No." I frowned. "I'm clearly a spectacular failure at this. Baker, I'm not even going to guess, so let me have it."

Sing glared at him. "He smokes too much—"

"I have a diagnosis. It's a horrible disease called LTP."

Abbey crinkled her nose. "I don't think I know that one."

"Likes To Party syndrome, bro."

Abbey slapped him on the arm. I studied Baker. He was laughing at his own joke, but there was something less than jovial about the tired look in his eyes.

"Seriously, what is it?" I asked.

"Doctor Laura thinks I've got something called Generalized Anxiety Disorder."

"You don't seem like the overly anxious type to me," I said.

"That's what I told him," Sing said, smacking him on the other arm.

As we exited Big Burrito, the discussion turned to our group homework assignments.

"It's no use," Sing said, pitching the napkin she'd used to open the door into a nearby trash barrel. "I try every week to do one of these stupid homework assignments and end up getting more frustrated. Not that I really care, I'm perfectly happy not letting people screw up my life. Just feel like I'm letting Neyle down is all."

"I know what you mean." Abbey sighed. "I need, like, a food chaperone or something."

I grabbed her shoulders and spun her around. *That's it.*

She gasped, and I realized I hadn't said the words aloud.

"That's it," I shouted.

A confused smile stretched her lips.

"What's it?" Luther looked confused, as I dragged him in front of Abbey and Sing.

"Abbey, you're a genius." I hugged her properly this time.

Sing raised her foot like she was prepared to kick me if I tried the same with her.

Abbey blushed. "Thanks?"

I laughed. They weren't following me, but they would soon enough.

"We've been going about this all wrong. There's a stupid cliché in sports: *There's no I in team.* Well, it isn't stupid. Not for us."

"But this isn't sports. It's our lives," Sing said, her eyes narrowed into dangerously sharp slits.

"Right, but I see no reason we can't apply a little team effort to our problems. Neyle never said this wasn't a group assignment. Let's help each other—"

"It *is* called group counseling, bro," Baker said, his tone sounding almost interested, which translated to excitement coming from him.

Abbey bit her lip. "I'm not sure, Ernie."

"But you said so yourself. If you only had a food chaperone, someone to help, you might be able to make it through a week without a setback. I'm going to help you." I looked at them individually. "I'm going to help all of you, and you're going to help each other."

Sing glanced at Baker, crinkling her nose. "This sounds like a tsunami of fail waiting to happen."

"C'mon, Sing. Hear me out. Everyone, I want you to go home tonight and think about what you'd like to accomplish. Meet me at the study rooms in the library tomorrow at evening at eight. It'll be dead then. We'll come up with a plan to do it. Together."

"You know what you're doing?" Luther asked as the others dispersed.

I grinned. "No clue, but it's going to be fun."

The next night, Sing, Abbey, Luther and I gathered at a long table in one of the study rooms. These were designated talking areas where groups could gather to work without fear of being shushed by the library staff. I stood by the whiteboard at one end of the room, where I stood to address the group.

Poise. Control. Authority. I tried to channel the best qualities of every coach I'd had.

"Thank you all for coming—Crap. Where's Baker?"

Luther shook his head. He had a baseball hat on, pushing his glasses down his nose further than usual.

The door to the room squeaked open.

"Sorry. Got lost." Baker's extra-baggy jeans scuffed the floor as he walked to his seat.

Sing glared. "The library is the biggest building on campus and you're a junior. How could you not know where it is?"

"It's a big campus." Baker shrugged.

"That's cool. We were only getting started," I said. "You'll recall, I asked everyone to come with something they'd like to achieve by the end of the semester. Who'd like to share theirs first?"

When no one volunteered, I pointed at Baker.

"No way."

"You were late, so you go first. Up here."

I sat as Baker walked to the front. He pulled a badly wrinkled piece of paper from his back pocket. He leaned close to me. "You suck, bro."

I gave him the thumbs up sign.

"My name is Baker, and I'd like to go an entire week without missing a class. And maybe smoke a little less ... but mostly go to class or whatever."

"Dream big," Luther said.

Baker flipped him the finger on the way to his seat.

I sighed. "Good, next."

Luther stood. "I'm Luther, and I'd like to show my father I'm not a failure because I couldn't join the military."

"Why couldn't you join the military?"

"They don't care for asthmatics. Which is ridiculous, because I can do all of the pushups and sit-ups. I need the occasional puff on my inhaler before I run is all. Because I've got a prescription, I'm not fit for service. Dad never believed I could even pass the tests."

How in the world would we make his dad see that?

"Abbey, and I want to eat something I know is bad for me." Her eyes blazed with excitement. "Like, pepperoni pizza or a hot dog."

"Fully," Baker said, looking as thrilled at the prospect as Abbey.

"And I don't want to feel guilty about it afterward. You know, like, not skip food for a week or barf." Abbey sat and took a sip from a sports bottle filled with a green liquid.

Sing crossed her arms and stared at the whiteboard. We waited.

"I'd like to be able to tolerate being in close proximity to people. Just for an hour or two maybe. That's it."

She'd mumbled through most of it, so I asked her to repeat for the sake of the others.

"I said I'd like to hang out with people and have fun doing it. See, like right now, I'm ready to throat-punch Baker and kick you in the soft parts for making me be here. I want the opposite of *this*." She held her arms out wide.

Baker scooted his chair further away from her, which wasn't an entirely unwarranted thing to do, gauging the malice brewing in Sing's chestnut-colored eyes.

"Okay." I took a dry erase marker from the tray below the whiteboard. "We've got eight weeks left in the semester. Each of you gets a week—"

"What about you?" Luther asked.

"Yeah, bro. What about you?"

"It's only fair we help you, too," Abbey said.

Sing smirked. "What do you want our help with, Ernie? If it's not being a pain in my ass, I'll gladly pitch in."

I scratched my head. There were lots of things I'd thought about. Apologizing to coach and the rest of my teammates, writing a letter to my dad in prison and confess how much I hated his guts, and other things I'd pretty much have to do on my own, if they ever got done.

"For once, I'd like to feel good about something I've done. I want to put someone else's wellbeing ahead of mine."

I stared at my new friends. Their faces were a mixture of hope and skepticism, which exactly reflected the struggle I'd been waging lately. The corners of my eyes stung.

"Let me help you guys, please. *This* is what I need to do."

They nodded their agreement, and so began our quest.

Chapter Twelve

The next morning, I slunk through the locker rooms of the Bo Price Fieldhouse, the campus athletic facility, feeling very much like the desperate hero traversing a dragon-infested swamp. And for anyone who'd ever stepped inside the men's locker room, swamp was definitely a fair comparison. The area was dank and had only two smells, fart or cologne. So much so that we'd taken to posting fake air quality alerts. A red piece of paper taped to the door meant someone had just taken a dump. Yellow indicated roughly fifteen minutes of tolerance before the stench would overwhelm. Green meant freshly cleaned.

I stood inside an empty shower stall and listened. No sign of Coach. *Perfect.* I crept on to the next one.

I'd snuck in through the emergency exit in the basement. I was hoping to find my target in the locker room so I wouldn't have go near the coaches' offices upstairs. Having been officially banished from the facility, it wouldn't do to have the Walrus catch me. He'd scorch my hero's ass for sure.

I spotted Bash hosing himself with body spray in front of one of the mirrors.

I ducked into a shower stall. "Pssst."

He turned, and went back to buttering his armpits with roll-on and watching his pecs dance in the mirror. He was one of the only guys on the team skinnier than me, so of course he looked ridiculous. I frowned and grabbed a bar soap. I nailed him in the back with it.

"Hey—"

"Bash, over here." I poked my head out again and waved.

He squinted. "Ernie?"

"Anyone else down here with you?"

He glanced around. "Nope."

I hopped out of the shower.

Bash met me with a high five and pulled me in for a quick man-hug. "Thought I was going to have to kick some ass. Hey, man. That wasn't cool of Junk to pull at the party the other night—"

"Never mind that. Have you seen Johnson?"

"Big? Yeah, he was upstairs lifting a little while ago. Why?"

Damn. The Walrus *loved* to lord over the weight room. Counting reps and then "accidentally" losing count so you'd have start over was his version of Saturday morning cartoons. I could almost hear him laughing in my head.

"Back to one, Demps. Back to one."

"Needed to talk to him about something, and I'm trying to avoid the Walrus. Don't suppose you'd go up and send him down for me?"

"No can do. I'll be late for my nine o'clock if I don't get out of here. Sorry, man."

"Thanks anyway."

I could camp in the locker room and hope he'd eventually come down, which might never happen. A lot of the guys would come in for a few minutes between classes, do a few sets, and then bolt for their next class without showering. And Big was pretty hardcore, so it wouldn't be that odd for him. I could wait for someone else to come down and see if they'd get him for me. A dangerous plan, because the next person I came across could easily be a coach, not to mention I might miss Big altogether. I could leave and try to track him down elsewhere, but I had no clue where he lived, didn't share any classes with him, and didn't hang in the same circles socially. Last option, I could go upstairs and hope the Walrus was in a class or otherwise engaged.

Bash went to the sink and stashed his deodorant in his book bag. He slung the strap over his shoulder and gave me a fist bump on the way back by.

"Ernie, I was thinking..."

My lips puckered. "Yeah?"

Bash mussed his hair and smoothed his shirt with his hands, his attention focused anywhere but on me. "Maybe you could apologize to the Walrus and get back on the team. I mean, we all know it's bullshit, but—"

I grabbed his shoulder. He finally turned his gaze on me. "We both know it's more complicated than that."

He laughed. A sheepish grin stretched his thin face. "Nah, you're right. We miss you around here."

I returned his smile, but the expression felt lifeless on my face. "I miss you guys, too."

I waited for him to leave. The room was quiet. Water dripped from one of the showerheads in random sequences. *Drip, drop, drip. Drop, drop, drip.* A musty odor tinged with the unnatural tangy smell of body spray hung heavy as fog in the air. *Definitely a yellow.* The overhead florescent lights painted the walls a dingy grayish shade, and created dizzying reflections off the shiny, metal paper towel dispensers. Cleats and sneakers peeked out of cubbies above the lockers, and strings dangled down like tiny jungle vines.

Pearls of cold sweat popped up on my forehead. I tugged at the collar of my shirt, trying to get some more air flow.

I missed my teammates. But, this place was now alien to me. I'd never been an unwelcome visitor in a locker room in all my life. This was no longer my domain, at least for the time being. I jogged to the door, eager to put the closing walls behind me.

I pulled my hoodie up to hide my face, and maneuvered down the glossy, lacquered hallways as quickly as I could. I paused by the trophy case in the main entrance. Two decades worth of baseball plaques dominated the display. A slowly aging Walrus flanked each of the team photos. It was easy to see why they'd named the Fieldhouse after him.

I continued on until I heard metal clanking together, then I grabbed the handle of one of the double doors and peeked into one of the rectangular windows. The wire security mesh made scoping the room difficult, but I didn't see any coaches.

Big was doing squats at the far end of the room. As I approached, Big's leg muscles, like slabs of layered granite, danced with each dip toward the floor. He yelled each time he pushed the weight back up. His spotter, a guy I didn't recognize, barked out the rep count. Sweat flooded from Big's cleanly shaved head, down to his bulging, sleeveless South State shirt, and puddled on the rubber floor around him. Big was an animal for sure, but also a fantastic first baseman. Good glove with a monster bat.

He was also the only guy on the team I hated to pitch to when I threw batting practice. If I ever got one a little too close to him, he'd try to rocket the next pitch back at the mound. He'd actually cracked the pitcher's screen we used to protect us during practice once. I'd beaned him for that one, and I was never so glad to have coaches around. Big would have detached my head from my shoulders if he could have gotten to me.

"'Sup, Big?" I glanced around. We were still alone.

He growled. After doing two more reps, he let his spotter help him offload the weight.

He snatched a towel to mop his head. "Hey."

We were both men of few words, which made most of our interactions somewhat strained and *very* brief.

"I don't have much time, and you seem busy, so I'll get to it. You still do the Army ROTC thing, right?"

He nodded and grinned. "Don't tell me you're signing up."

"Don't think I've got what it takes, huh?" I laughed, because I knew what his answer would be.

"No offense, Ernie, but you've got the self-discipline of a hyper two year old. If you can't stay on the college baseball team—as the star player no less—you got no chance in the military."

I slapped him on the arm. "No argument there. Actually, I'm asking for a friend. I need a favor."

He crossed his arms and glared, which I guessed meant he was listening. *A good start.*

Big and I quickly concluded our business and I headed out. The wall of glass doors shimmered before me. Confidence flowed through my veins right along with the oxygen. Twenty more feet and I'd have infiltrated the Walrus's domain, accomplished my task, and vanished without him being the wiser. Super-spy Ernie Demps had a nice ring to it—

"Hold on a second," a too familiar voice called out.

I froze.

After I'd been screamed at enough by someone, his or her voice had a way of hardwiring into my brain and triggering an almost autonomic emotional response. Fear, shame, happiness, and anger could be triggered with a word. Mom had been dead for years, but I could still hear my mom chastising me for having a "clean clothes pile" instead of using drawers and hangers. Like broken glass being raked over a chalkboard, the sound, even in my memory, was unbearably annoying. The Walrus's voice was in there right along with hers.

My heart tumbled around in my chest like it had come loose. *Run like hell!* A childish, panicking voice pleaded in my head. I took two more steps toward the doors.

"Can't we talk about it?"

His voice was more fragile than I'd ever heard it. Was he actually asking — not telling — me to do something? My mouth was open, but I was way too confused to say anything.

I'd resolved to turn and face him when a lightening bolt in the form of a redheaded graduate student struck by me.

"Margery, wait," the Walrus said from some distance behind me.

I cinched my hoodie a little tighter and followed her into the daylight.

Chapter Thirteen

I walked behind Margery for a long while. Her now-familiar ponytail swished from side to side as she marched over the sidewalks crisscrossing campus. She wore a black floral-patterned dress that ended just above her calves. A simple, red wool cardigan covered her torso. In contrast to the otherwise very feminine garb, she wore a pair of rubber-soled white walking shoes.

Her look pretty well summed my opinion of her to this point. She was a chocolate covered almond: sweet and maybe a touch indulgent on the outside, hard and practical on the inside.

Her vibrant sweater clashed with the bank of gray clouds pushing the sunlight from the sky on the horizon. We were in for a stormy night ahead. Not that unusual for mid-spring in Southern Illinois.

After I'd followed long enough to make sure the Walrus wasn't chasing after, I trotted beside her.

"Wait up."

She gasped. "You startled me. Sorry."

Her brow was creased with worry lines.

"I can leave you with your thoughts if you want. I saw you leaving the Fieldhouse, and thought maybe I could return the favor of a friendly ear."

"Thanks."

We resumed walking. "You and your dad have it out?"

Her head snapped around. "He's infuriating. How do you play for someone like him?"

I snorted. "You might've noticed I'm not all that successful at it."

"Right." She smirked.

"Coach isn't all bad. He knows baseball, and I respect him for that. He's simply not a great negotiator. But that's no different than any other coach I've had. Someone has to lead, and whoever that is needs to have the last word on most things."

"I suppose, but at some point, you have to acknowledge there's a world outside of what you control." Her fists balled. "Like today. I went to his office to inform him that some of his players were in danger of failing my class if they didn't show up for the quizzes. Dr. Ben had apparently been looking the other way. You know what my father said to me?"

I shook my head and considered throwing my hands up to deflect a punch. She was that pissed.

"'They're ball players, Margie, not poets. Couldn't you get them by somehow? Maybe let 'em write an essay or something to make it up.' Can you believe that?"

I pulled my hood down and scuffed my hair, hoping to straighten it. "Actually, yeah."

"You're a jerk."

She shoved me sideways, but at least she was smiling now.

"You're right. I'm probably expecting too much of him," she said.

"No."

I drifted back beside her. We were close enough our shoulders rubbed about every third step. Each touch set off a surge of nervous excitement in my brain. I didn't fail to notice she wasn't trying to create more space between us, creating a different kind of thrill. She clearly no longer despised me. If we were diplomats engaged in wartime peace talks, I think we'd have labeled this as *progress*.

"Expectations are a good thing," I said. "I've lived most of my life not worrying about what others wanted from me. I'm starting to see what a mistake that was. You need to be something for someone other than yourself, or you're really nothing at all."

She studied me with a bemused smile. "I've told you you're weird, right?"

"You might've mentioned it the other night." I stared down at my feet.

"About that—"

"I won't say a word."

"It's not that." She sighed and nodded to a concrete bench off the path ahead. "Got a second?"

"Absolutely." I lied.

My eleven o'clock chemistry class had kicked off. But I was more interested in the un-scientific kind of chemistry at the moment.

We settled on the seat. A pair of flowering shrubs perched on either side shielded us from the sidewalk traffic for the most part. Bees hummed between the pink buds. The air was laced with a strong, floral scent.

Margery placed her hands in her lap. Sunlight reflected off of her ruby-colored glasses as she looked up at me. "I want to apologize. That should never have happened."

"But it did," I said, unable to keep a grin off of my face.

Her cheeks reddened. "Yes, it did. And while I enjoyed spending time with you, it was *very* unprofessional of me."

She'd been thinking about it, too. "You're still a student here. So am I. People meet at parties. I don't think it has to be a big deal."

"But that's just it," she said. My hand rested on the bench between us. She traced her fingers across my skin for a moment. I was glad the touch came on the top of my hand, because my palms were slicked with sweat. "This *could* be a big deal. Even if it's by accident, I'm teaching one of your classes now. There are ethical considerations. We're a small college that doesn't really have positions for graduate teaching assistants.

Dr. Ben got a grant for me to be able to help him with his research and do some administrative stuff for his classes. They're letting me fill in for him because I've been in the program a while, and it's too late in the semester to cancel the class. None of the other professors could cover it. I want to get my PhD down the road, and this could go a long way toward getting me into a program. It's a big opportunity for me, and I can't screw it up over a silly crush."

"You've got a crush on me?"

"Wha—what? That's not what I meant." She folded her arms.

I rubbed my ear. "Nope, working fine. Definitely sounded like you meant it."

"You're delusional."

"That's not my official diagnosis, but I assume there's room to grow into it."

"Shit. I'm sorry." She took her glasses off and rubbed her nose. "That was completely insensitive."

"You *do* have a potty mouth." I laughed, and put my hand on top of hers. "It's cool. Really. But so what if it is a crush? It's allowed. Even encouraged in some settings, like, college."

She yanked her hand back. "Don't be ridiculous. We'd been drinking, and we're clearly not compatible—"

"You'd been drinking. I was stone sober. And who says we're not compatible?"

"I do—" Her eyes bulged. "Wait. You weren't drunk?"

"Nope."

"You took advantage of me."

She smacked my arm, but her smile told me she wasn't all that disturbed by the idea.

"Maybe a little. Listen..." I lowered my voice. "I know you hate baseball players. I know you're taking a huge risk. But I like you. A lot. We can be discrete, but please give me a chance to get to know you. Get to know me. I told you before, I'm not who you think I am."

"I'm *really* starting to see that. Trust me. The real you is much more persistent and annoying than I would've ever given you credit for." She sighed. "It's not a great idea."

"But it's an idea," I said.

My pulse quickened. If I couldn't convince her now, I'd never be able to.

My phone vibrated in my pocket. *Damn.* It was the alarm for my chemistry lab. I could miss all of the lectures I wanted, but the labs were a huge part of my grade.

I hopped up from the bench. "I've got to make this next class. Say you'll give me a chance."

"Ernie, I'm—"

"No one will know if you don't want them to. I'll grovel right here."

I fell to my knees on the grass in front of her and held my arms out to the sky.

"Get up." She scanned to see if anyone was watching. "You're impossible."

I nodded my agreement and waddled closer to her.

"Fine, yes. Get up," she said. "People are staring."

"Good. What time do you get home tonight?" I leapt to my feet.

"Tonight? No. Absolutely not, I've got things to do."

I took a few steps away from her. "You might have to shout it if I get much further."

She rolled her eyes. "Fine. Six o'clock."

I rang Margery's doorbell at six sharp. Somewhere in the sullen sky, the sun waned toward night, but it had been mostly dark for thirty minutes or more. Rain wasn't falling yet, but the echo of distant thunder told me a storm was coming.

She answered the door with a rye smile on her face. "You're punctual. I'll give you that."

She stepped aside. Her hair was down. The first time I'd seen it that way. Natural, strawberry-hued curls danced around her shoulders and over her face. I wanted to run my fingers through them in the worst way but opted to follow her into a small living room instead.

"Any roommates?" I sat on the edge of an oversized ottoman.

"Just me. Don't get any ideas." She wandered into a nearby room. "What can I get you to drink? Beer? Water?"

"I'm good. Thanks."

"I'll get my shoes and I'll be ready for … well, whatever it is you've got planned."

"Grab a raincoat," I warned.

She poked her head around a doorway. Her eyes narrowed. "We're not going to be outside, are we?"

"No, but my motorcycle doesn't have a roof."

"We're taking your motorcycle?" Her voice went up an octave. "I could drive—"

"We'll be perfectly safe. Maybe not dry, but safe. Promise."

She pointed at me, letting her weight shift so that her hips pushed to one side. "It's the dry part I'm worried about. Mostly."

"Consider this our first trust exercise. You'll be wearing a helmet—no one will see. Just get your things." I sent her away with a flip of my hand.

I scanned the room. Simply framed vinyl record sleeves dotted the walls. There were newer bands, like Muse and My Chemical Romance, and some oldies, like the Stones and the Beatles. I stood to inspect one nearest me.

"You like?" Margery slipped into a pair of low-heeled sandals. The pale skin between the waistline of her jeans and the bottom of her tank top flashed as she shimmied. Her green eyes stayed focused on mine as she hopped from one leg to the other. One of the straps on her shirt fell, exposing a freckled shoulder.

"Yes." I coughed to clear my head as much as my throat. "I mean, they're cool."

"I've got a pretty good collection now. You'll have to come over and listen with me sometime." She slid into a jacket and smiled. "Ready?"

I nodded, moving closer to her. "I want to give you something first."

She bit her lip. "Okay?"

"Carrying flowers on the bike is kind of difficult, but I wanted to commemorate our first date somehow."

I pulled a piece of paper from the inside pocket of my jacket and unfolded it. She reached for the page. I yanked it back.

"Hey," she said, pursing her lips in a mock-pout. "Is it mine or not?"

"I'll read it to you. It's called Burned Out Stars Do Brightly Shine"

Time calls, we must heed,
Yet the watchers above are free.
A slipping step, a bold move,
All they see.
 Stars shine, sometimes fall,
Twinkling, shimmering, and bold.
But those whose light is already gone,
Do burn brightest of all.

Margery clapped. "It's beautiful. Who wrote it?"

A deep breath swelled my chest as relief and pride rushed into me.

"It's mine." I handed her the paper. "Now it's yours."

Chapter Fourteen

Margery placed her glowing, neon orange golf ball on the black floor. The silhouette of her body stood out against the bright obstacles of the putt-putt course around us. The steady, thumping rhythm of a pop song I didn't recognize blared in the cavernous indoor space.

"You know," she said, lining up her shot. "When you promised no one would find out, I didn't think you meant our date would literally be in the dark."

"I'm a man of my word." I came up behind her. "Jurassic Golf is a local legend. How have you *not* been here before?"

"It's called studying."

"Well, this is called fun." I wrapped my arms around her, and placed my hands over her forearms. "Remember, one fluid motion … don't let anything break your focus."

"Quiet on the green. And how about some room?" She gave me a playful elbow in the ribs to separate us. "You clearly aren't paying attention. I don't need your help. If I get par on this one, I win."

"Not if I've lost the scorecard."

"You better not have."

Her teeth were blindingly white in the black lights as she smiled. She pointed the club in my direction. The glowing head pecked me in the chest and pushed me farther away.

"It's pretty dark, who knows what might happen to it." I held the paper out in front of me.

Margery focused on her ball again. "Who knows what'll happen to *you* if you lose it."

An animatronic T-Rex roared in the distance. She gave the golf ball a solid tap, and it rolled up and over the first hump. We trotted alongside to watch its progress as it scuttled over the long tail of the dinosaur. Up and down it went, then it bounced off the radiant course barriers. When the ball reached the head of the lizard, it dropped in a hole there. By the time we made our way down the short stairway to where we thought the ball would come out of the dinosaur's belly, it was gone.

Margery huffed. "What the hell?"

The laughter died in my throat with terrible realization. She'd sunk the damned thing.

"No way." I walked over to the cup, which had a pink glow-in-the-dark ring around it.

I picked up the ball and handed it over to Margery.

"My first ever hole in one." She thrust her trophy ball in my face. "I win."

"Yes, you're the champion of children's, glowing golf," I said. "Let's get you your winner's milkshake from the snack bar, Tiger."

We shared ice cream, talked poetry, laughed about her dad, played glow-in-the-dark pinball, and generally enjoyed each other's company for a couple of hours. The place was filled with families and tweens, so we didn't even have to worry too much about being seen by anyone who knew us.

As we cruised down the road, only a few blocks from her house, I looked forward to telling her how great a time I'd had. A blinding, white light split the sky in front of us. I swerved, but managed to keep control of the bike as the first sheet of rain slammed into us. Another burst of rain came, propelled by a gale-force wind that threatened to sweep the motorcycle out from under us. Then, all of the moisture in the air seemed to release at once, and it was like driving under a continuous waterfall. Water ran down the gutters of the street in a raging river, keeping me from parking at the curb. I sped up to be able to cruise into her drive. We hit the flowing rainwater fast, forcing two huge waves into the air on either side, further soaking us. By the time we'd skidded to a stop beneath her carport, we both shook so violently from the chill of the soaking I had to steady her purse so she could fish her keys out.

We entered the house through a side door and into a tiny mudroom. I held my arms above my head, clamping my teeth together to keep them from chattering as icy water ran from my head, over my back, and eventually pooled on the tiled floor. Margery faced me, her hair plastered to the side of her head, her clothes drooping from her body like extra skin. Dark streaks of eyeliner lined her cheeks.

"What … the … fuck-was-that-all-about?" She cried out and stomped on the tiles. I didn't know if she was trying to warm up, shake the water from her bones, or if she was simply throwing a fit.

I couldn't articulate anything, so I laughed.

She glared at me, but her frustration eventually gave way to laughter, too. We stayed there, drip-drying and laughing, for a few minutes. Eventually, she kicked off her soggy shoes and told me to stay put. She returned a couple of minutes later, wearing sweats, and had a towel wrapped around her head.

"Here."

She tossed me my own towel, and a fluffy pink robe covered with bloodshot-eyed blue bunnies drinking coffee. I held the garment out in front of me and arched my eyebrows. *Had to be a sick joke…*

She shrugged. "Either ditch the wet clothes and put on the robe, or stand there and freeze to death. I'm making tea."

She winked and left. I put my wet clothes in the dryer and slid into the robe. It barely covered my thighs. But it *was* warm. Margery lit a compressed paper log in the fireplace as I entered. When she spotted me, she put down the lighter and covered her mouth with her hand.

"You look *fabulous.*"

I curtsied and sneered. "Glad I can entertain. Although, I'm a bit disappointed there weren't cat slippers."

"Oh, you're definitely entertaining. And I'm sure I can find the slippers. Tea is on the table, handsome."

Rain bombarded the windows and roof, creating a

muted, drumming chorus. Margery went to a bookcase filled with records. As she perused her collection, I sat on the floor in front of the fireplace and sipped my tea. The thought of fire heated me as much as the actual flames.

"Like Charlie Parker?" she asked.

"Not sure."

She gasped as if I'd kicked a puppy into the mouth of a hungry, waiting lion. A minute later, the crackling sound of the record spinning joined the sounds of the falling rain. Strings swelled, and then a saxophone honked out the opening notes to the old jazz standard, *Summertime*. Warm and buttery smooth, it was the musical equivalent of a favorite blanket.

Margery plopped down next to me, humming along with Parker. I moved my toes to the rhythm. She grinned. "Like Charlie Parker now?"

"Still not sure." I inched closer to her.

Our body heat combined to give me the first real feeling of warmth I'd had since coming in out of the rain. She touched my bare knee below the hem of the robe. A new sensation burned, this one from within.

"Now?" she whispered.

"He's growing on me."

I cupped her face in my hand, tilting her head up to meet mine. Her lips were moist from the tea, and I could taste a hint of the honey she'd used to sweeten it. We kissed an eternity of seconds, only pausing to gulp in short breaths. I ran my hands through her hair, then over her shoulders, and finally down her torso to her hips. She raised her arms to let me pull the sweatshirt over her head and still-damp hair. Her naked flesh prickled with goose bumps, so I opened my robe and pulled her body against mine. She arched her back and let me guide her to the floor.

Our mouths connected again. Her teeth nipped at the soft flesh of my bottom lip, creating twinges of pleasurable pain. Sharp fingernails traced playfully over my back as my hands massaged the outsides of her thighs, then the insides. Her moans grew increasingly urgent as I explored the softest areas of her body with my fingers. My pulse raced with the sounds of her pleasure. She climaxed and an electric tingle seemed to pass from her body to mine. I had to be with her—

Oh shit. Condom. I pulled away from her probing hands.

"What is it?" Her tone was urgent.

"I ... I don't have protection."

She bit her lip, pushing my desire to taste them again through the roof. "Check your robe pocket."

I patted frantically and smiled when I heard the wrapper crinkle. "Why, Ms. Price. If I didn't know any better, I'd say you had planned on seducing me all along."

She grinned. "Just put it on."

At last, she wrapped her legs around my waist, yanking me fully on top of her. I smoothed the hair away from her face so I could look her in the eyes as our bodies joined for the first time.

Afterward, we lay curled together in front of the dwindling sparks of the artificial log. Our discarded clothes formed a makeshift blanket beneath us. The cold from the rain had left entirely, replaced by the pleasant radiating heat only two bodies so closely mingled can create. I kissed little patterns on her shoulders and arms, enjoying the way her skin flashed pink and then quickly returned to its smooth, milky whiteness with each press of my lips.

Margery reached her hand back and gently tugged at my hair until I brought my probing mouth to meet hers once again. When we parted, she let out a satisfied sigh. The last song on the album ended, and the record came to a static-filled stop.

Her eyelids fluttered open. "*Now* what do you think of Mr. Parker?"

I pulled her back to me. "He's my new favorite."

Chapter Fifteen

"You're smiling again." Luther put his pen down.

I chewed on mine. "Was I?"

He crisscrossed his arms, and rested his back against the video game poster behind him. "Yes, and it's a little unnerving. We've been at this for an hour, and everything we've come up with could either get us killed or expelled." He threw his hands in the air. "I see nothing to smile about."

I grinned again, more to mess with him this time. "It'll be fine. I think the plan for Abbey seems reasonably safe."

His frown told me he didn't share my positive take, but he couldn't know that I'd had one of the best weeks of my life. Since Junk had nearly choked me to death, things had taken a turn for the better. The result made me feel as if the world had very few obstacles left for me—at least that I could see. It even made spending a rainy Saturday morning in Luther's dorm room feel like a nice retreat.

Margery and I had slept very little after Thursday night's escapade. She'd had a paper to work on, so we shared some toast and coffee, and I let myself out while she showered — which had been an exquisitely difficult thing to do, in retrospect. Since then, I'd been in a state of dizzy euphoria. I should have been exhausted when I fell onto my bed in the dorm Friday morning, but my body and brain seemed to be begging me to not let what they'd experienced end. So I went to all of my classes by default.

"Yeah," Luther said, yanking me out of my happy place, "until you factor in she has a serious eating disorder and we could trigger some kind of breakdown."

"Well, there's that, but we're not going to let that happen." I clapped him on the shoulder. "We're a team now. Hard times and good times. We share the burden of failure and the joy of success together, or not at all."

Luther uncrossed his arms. "You make us sound like the Ninja Turtles. I'm going to use that line in my next clan meeting, by the way."

He pulled his phone from a pocket on his camouflaged cargo pants and tapped the screen.

I knew Luther liked the idea of us being some kind of well-oiled machine, working toward a unified goal. But I didn't have the heart to tell him our team was more of a broken down antique that we'd probably end up pushing across the finish line — if we crossed at all. However, I thought I'd better save that pep talk for later.

My mind was too filled with thoughts of Margery for troubles, anyway. We hadn't spent time together since *the night*, but we'd texted each other a few times. I was sure I really, *really* liked her. In fact, I'd never been so captivated by a girl. Ever. She was mature, smart, had incredible taste in music, redefined my concept of beauty, and swore more than I did. I also figured I could safely assume she was into me—enough to get involved even when she knew it could cause her problems professionally.

But I still didn't know her all that well. When I thought too long about things, a ghost of doubt haunted me. Maybe this *was* only infatuation—for both of us. She'd eventually come to her senses and end up with a guy on her level. One who wouldn't cost her the teaching gig she'd dreamed of for so long. Maybe she'd suddenly realize that beneath the poetry and charm, I was still a baseball player. Something I knew didn't sit well with her. Sure, I saw things the other way around, but I might have been too much of one over the other for her taste.

I decided not to push things along too quickly. I would hold off on calling her until Sunday. Not that I wouldn't spend every free second of my day in her company if she allowed me. I didn't want to screw this up, which would fit the pattern of my life a little too well.

"Baker is easy," Luther said. "We follow him around to class for a week, right?"

"And maybe use pizza as bait."

Luther sighed. "You're getting goofy. You need a video game break to focus."

"Now you're talking," I said.

He leapt off of his bed and fired up his forty-inch flat screen. The TV rested on his desk, and the screen took up the entire wall space between the bed and a small sink. Corkboard lined the wall behind the monitor, but Luther only used the top couple of inches, pinning passwords and usernames to it.

He connected a cable to his laptop, pressed a few keys, and a car racing game came up. Luther tossed me a controller, and while he was getting things set up, I fished a can of potato chips out of my book bag for us to share.

"You'll have to explain the controls." I took a can of soda he'd pulled from his mini-fridge and offered me.

"S'easy. Use the sticks to steer and the buttons on top for gas and brakes."

He held up his controller and demonstrated. I might have missed something, because I wrapped my car around a tree within the first thirty seconds of the race.

"It's easy," I said, mocking his matter-of-fact tone.

He grinned, tilting his body into every turn as if he were really driving. "You're an athlete and drive a motorcycle. You should have the ideal reflexes for this."

Luther sideswiped my car with his, slamming me through a fence and into a field full of grazing cows.

"When I drive a motorcycle, people aren't usually trying to kill me, asshole."

He cackled and rammed another car in front of him.

"You've got issues," I said.

"That's what Neyle tells me," he said, sending us both into a fit of laughter.

I finished in last place and demanded an instant rematch.

"So who is going to be our hardest case in the group?" I

asked, leaning into a curve with my car.

"Sing," Luther said. "She's so touchy, and absolutely routine driven. We won't get her out of her dorm unless we get it on her schedule six months in advance, much less make her socialize with other people."

"Maybe we'll have to go to her then. Next."

Luther furrowed his brow. "Me?"

"How do you figure?"

"You don't know my dad, Ernie. You can't reason with him. If he doesn't see something with his own eyes, it doesn't happen or exist. Getting him to believe I'm not worthless … I don't know how. And trust me, I've spent a lot of time thinking about it."

I nodded, making a mental note about the "seeing is believing" dilemma. Something told me dealing with his father would be like handling a loaded gun. But Luther had to face him at some point, and I'd resolved to be by his side when he did.

"Next."

"Abbey."

"Baker's already helping me with that one." I tried to knock Luther's controller out his hands so he wouldn't win, *again*, but he still crossed the finish line ahead of one of the computer-controlled cars. I finished last, again.

"How is Baker going to help?" The ugly way he scrunched up his nose and glasses when he said it showed Luther's skepticism-to-trust ratio was about three to one. Not in Baker's favor, I guessed.

"He's on it. You really need to have more faith in

Baker."

"Said the guy who hasn't had to track him down a million times to remind him what day it is."

I laughed. "Touché. Speaking of Baker, I guess that leaves him."

"We need to make sure he gets to class. Maybe we can do up a schedule, take turns walking him. Then someone will have to get him out of bed every morning. Easy."

I shook my head. "We're going to have to do better than that."

Luther paused the game. "How?"

"Do you know where he gets his weed?" My eyes widened. "He doesn't grow it, does he?"

That would be an entirely different kind of problem.

"No, only smokes. I'm pretty sure he gets his from the same person most of the campus buys from. A guy named Buzz. Biology major, I think. Why?"

The pieces of my plan for Baker finally clicked into place. I only needed to track down a drug dealer first.

"Think you can put a schedule together for Baker's classes? Get it to Sing and Abbey?"

"Sure," Luther said. "What about getting him up in the mornings?"

"I'll take care it." I put the game controller down and gathered my things. "And the weed."

My search for Buzz led me to the campus greenhouse.

Naturally. He was one of the students who helped care for the plants the Biology Club raised and sold for fundraising. I'd gotten in touch with one of my former teammates who enjoyed the occasional toke. He, *of course*, knew Buzz and, *of course*, offered to let me smoke with him. I politely declined, but asked if he could track down his dealer for me. My lie was simple. I was looking to score some for a party. A few texts were sent, and we learned Buzz was at the greenhouse.

The air inside the glass building was steamy and only slightly less moist than the air outside—and it was still raining. There were five long rows of plants. Some were overgrown, and some only getting started. Still more hung from metal rods that intersected the ceiling above, giving the place the feel of a neatly organized jungle. I made my way down the first aisle, being careful not to trip over the water hoses snaking across the path at my feet. I sneezed.

"You got allergies, too?" a male voice called to me from the next row.

I rounded the corner. A guy the size of a baby elephant delicately snipped spent buds from a plant. He had lilac purple, elbow-length gardening gloves on.

"Buzz?"

He extended his hand for me to shake. I glanced at his glove.

"My bad." He removed the glove and offered his hand again. "Don't know where mine went so I had to swipe a pair from a girl's locker."

I shook his hand. Below a dingy mop of blond hair, a pair of very red eyes took me in. Somehow, I doubted allergies were the source of his troubles.

"You here to buy a plant? We've got some really nice azaleas coming along."

"Actually, I'm not sure if you have the plants I'm looking for." I raised my eyebrows.

When he didn't reply, I added, "Here, that is."

I wanted to make sure he did what other people said he did before I got down to business.

He took a look around, then leaned close. "I don't do that here, but we can talk later. Let me give you my card—"

"Actually, I'm not interested in making a purchase exactly. I just wanted to make sure you're the right guy."

His eyes narrowed. "I don't know what you're talking about."

He turned his back to me and started pruning again.

I touched his shoulder. He jumped.

"Look, dude, I don't know who you're working for or whatever, but I got no clue what you're talking about."

"I don't work for anyone," I whispered. "And I'm not trying to get you in trouble."

"You're not?"

"No. I needed to talk to you about one of your clients."

"So that's what this is about." He poked me in the chest. "I don't rat on customers. You need to leave. Now"

His hands balled into fists that could have been confused for small, fleshy melons.

I took a step back. "Let's start over. I'm a friend of Baker's."

He unclenched his hands. "You're buds with Baker?"

"Yes, it's him I need to talk to you about."

"I'm listening…"

I explained how we were trying to help Baker, and how I thought taking a small smoke sabbatical might increase our chances of success.

"I don't know, man. Bake's my best customer."

"I can see that. Trust me. And I'm not asking you to quit doing business with him forever. That's Baker's choice."

"What makes you think he won't get it from someone else?"

"Does Baker strike you as the most motivated of guys? Besides, we're only trying to help him through this one week."

Buzz sat on a nearby stool with a huff. He bumped one of the large tables holding the plants and moved it an inch. "It might hurt his feelings if I cut him off for no reason."

I somehow doubted Baker's emotional state was first on Buzz's priority list, but whatever. "Tell him you had some kind of shortage. Bugs ate your crop, or you ran out. I don't know."

Buzz puffed out his already swollen chest. "I never run out."

I rubbed my eyes. Arguing with a drug dealer in a greenhouse was surprisingly absent from my bucket list. I'd have to come at this from a different angle. He wasn't selling drugs for the philanthropy of it, so maybe it was time to talk business with him.

"How much is it going to take?" I pulled out my wallet.

He scratched his head. "You're going to pay me to *not* sell weed to someone?"

"That's the idea. How much?"

"You're crazy."

I eyed him. "Probably. How much?"

He beamed like a fisherman who knew he had one on the line. Being on the receiving end of a hook wasn't the best feeling I'd ever had.

"Like I said, Baker is my top customer. Two hundred."

"For a week?" I was seriously going to have to have a talk with Baker about the volume of weed he was consuming. "Fifty."

"How about one hundred."

"How about we both remember we're college students, first. Seventy-five, and I forget to mention what you're doing to campus security should I ever cross paths with them."

Buzz frowned, but eventually stuck his hand out to seal the deal. Could I trust the drug dealing future botanist? Probably not, but it was the best I could do.

I yanked my hand away before we could shake. "Throw in a non-smokeable plant."

He groaned. "Sure, whatever, man."

Chapter Sixteen

The world was green, damp, and new after the recent storms. The smells of cleansed dirt and air overwhelmed, completing the total sensory overload. I rocked back and forth on my heels waiting for Margery to answer my knock. My arms were behind my back to conceal the gift I'd brought her.

The door cracked. One of Margery's emerald eyes peered out at me above the chain lock. The door closed, the chain slid back, and then the door opened fully. Her hips were thrust to one side, her arms knotted over her chest, and if her ponytail had been a cat's tail, I was sure it would have been twitching. In short, Margery was pissed.

"Hi?" I turned my head slightly as if to absorb a slap I hadn't yet received.

"Making the rounds this morning, are we?"

"I wanted to see you"

I watched her expression closely to see if I'd said the right thing. Her nostrils flared. I hadn't. She poked me in the chest.

"You own a phone, right? It works for things other than sending text messages, you know."

I swallowed back something hard and nodded. *Oh boy.*

"Perhaps you could warn a girl before popping over." She threw her hands up. "Or, *I don't know,* maybe give her a call after you've spent the night with her. Look, if this is how it's—"

"Can I come in, so we can talk about it?"

I scanned our surroundings. Thankfully, the neighborhood was mostly either still asleep or at church.

"No."

I flinched. "What do you mean, no?"

"I need to start teaching ESL courses." She put her hands on her waist and sighed. "I mean, no, you can't come in. You can say whatever you came by to say right here."

Note to self: Definitely call her next time.

"Okay, I'll have to give you these some other time."

"That's rig—wait. Give me what?"

"Oh, nothing." I took the first step down off of the porch.

She stood on her tiptoes trying to see around me. "Are those flowers?"

"Sort of." I grinned. She'd taken the bait. Now, it was my turn to play fisherman.

"For me?" Margery's face brightened with a broad smile.

I shrugged. "They were for the girl who lived here, who liked me enough to let me come inside. Guess she's not home, so…"

"Let me see them first. If they're pretty, I'll see if I can find her."

I laughed, holding the clay pot out in front of me. "You really are an evil person."

She nodded enthusiastically. "I know. Gimme."

I handed them over, and she stuck her nose to one of the delicate pink flowers. "They smell amazing."

"They're called Star Scent azaleas. I'm told they're especially fragrant."

Her eyes gleamed. "Where'd you get them?"

I scratched my head, debating whether I should tell her about my new pot-dealing gardener. "I know a guy."

She went inside and I followed. We sat at a little bistro table tucked into the corner of her kitchen.

I took her hand. "Sorry I didn't call. I didn't want to come off as pushy."

She smiled. "Ernie, if flowers and poetry is you being pushy, barrel over me. Please."

"I promised we'd try to be discrete."

"I know, and I appreciate it. But I'm okay with us spending time together." She studied me. "If you're okay with it."

"I believe I am, yes." I stood and walked to her side. Her head tilted back as she stared up at me, and I kissed her.

We spent the rest of the day together, much of it on the

couch with Margery's head in my lap. A continuous soundtrack of jazz greats played on the record player. Open windows let the birds sing along, and a steady breeze stirred the lacy curtains as we chatted. *Perfection.*

"You're a sophomore, right?" Margery tapped out the rhythm to the song we were listening to on my forearm with her fingers.

"For a few more weeks, at least."

"My God, you're young." She smirked mischievously. "You date a lot of dinosaurs?"

I squeezed her in my arms. "I don't date a lot in general. And there are only three years difference between us."

"Just saying, entire wars have been fought and lost in less time."

"And I'm *just saying…*" I tickled her ribs. "I don't lose a lot of wars."

"Stop that." She squirmed and swatted my hands away. "What are you going to do after college?"

I gazed at the ceiling, watching blades of sun dance across in little daggers as the bustling curtains shifted the shadows. "Assuming I don't lose my scholarship and get to actually finish?"

"You think Dad is really going to do it?"

I nodded. "He would have already if Coach Ramirez hadn't come to bat for me."

"You're going to counseling like he asked. And kicking his best pitcher off the team doesn't sound very much like something my dad would do unless at gunpoint. Growing up, he'd have traded me for a win."

"I think you're underestimating him. He hates me." I kissed her forehead. "And he'd have traded you to get out of an inning, much less for a win."

She smacked my cheek playfully. "Can I ask you something? About the other night—"

"Sure, but you might have to reenact some things to jog my memory." I wrapped my arm around her waist.

She flushed pink. "Not that. Yet. When we were together, I saw the tattoos on your back."

"The feathers." I hoped the frown I was feeling was more of the inside kind. This was a subject I wasn't quite ready to get into with her—or anyone, really. "Something dumb I did when I graduated high school. My nickname with the guys on the team is Hawk, so I thought some falling feathers would be cool. I'm pretty sure my buddy Junk got a dog collar inked in a place I hope to never see."

She smiled. "Well, I thought they were pretty. Finish telling me your plans."

I sighed, half in relief to be moving on from the tats. "I don't know, honestly. Baseball is all I've ever counted on doing. Beyond that, not sure."

"Think you can play professionally?"

"I actually got drafted out of high school. Not in the high rounds or anything, but the Kansas City Royals wanted me to play for their farm team in Arkansas. Would've jumped at the chance had it not been for a promise."

Margery sat up, taking my hand with her. "What promise?"

I let her pull me to a sitting position.

"Mom begged me to go to college if I ever had the opportunity. She was proud of me as a ball player. But always as a stepping-stone to getting an education, nothing else. She'd gotten pregnant with me and had to drop out of high school, and then ended up taking care of a drunk, abusive prick *and* baby Ernie. So she never got to use her brain the way she wanted. I think she fantasized about finding me in libraries studying for admittance into law school or something."

I chuckled but didn't feel as happy as the sound let on.

"So you went to college for her?"

"Near the end, when the cancer had taken everything away but her breath, I knelt beside her bed and promised her I'd get a degree if I could."

Margery kissed my hand. "That's sweet."

The memories of Mom further soured my thoughts. Even with one dead and the other in prison, my parents never stopped hounding me.

I pulled my hand away. "I think it was a stupid promise made by a sad kid. I didn't have any business going to college."

A crushing reality swept over me. In my mind, I'd already ended my promise to her. Getting kicked off the team was a first step in that direction, and now I was laying here seriously considering life outside of school.

"Don't be silly, you're a good student." She reached out to bring me back to the couch with her.

I stepped beyond her grasp. Suddenly, I didn't feel

very much like being touched.

"It's getting late. I've got some reading to do and need to get up early tomorrow."

"Ernie, are you okay? Did I say something to—"

"No."

I slid my shoes on and faced her. A look of confusion and hurt clouded her features.

"It's me." My chest tightened with the words. "You're perfect."

She followed me to the door. "I'm sorry. I shouldn't have brought it up."

I kissed her cheek. "It's just me. I'll be fine, really. See you in class?"

I put my helmet on and waved goodbye. A single phrase traced through my mind as I sped away. *It's always me.*

Chapter Seventeen

"Dr. Laura can see you now. But you'd better make an appointment next time," Angry said, cranking the volume back up on her tunes.

I could hear them blaring from her headphones when I walked by. Dr. Jones typed away as I entered.

"Ernie." She grinned. "This is a good surprise. Our next session wasn't for another week. Everything okay?"

I took the chair directly in front of her desk so she wouldn't have to come over to the couch. "Yeah, I think so."

She straightened. "No offense, but in my line of work *think so* usually translates to heck no. What's up?"

"You got me." I pulled at some loose strings on the cuff of my shirt, trying to coax the right words from my mouth. "I think I'm lost ... as a person."

"How so?"

"That's just it. I'm not sure. I came to you, understanding what I was all about. Not proud, but I understood. Since then, I've been going through some changes. I've met people — like the people in the group — who make me think I didn't really know much about myself then, and I know even less now."

She smiled. "Aristotle said knowing yourself is the beginning of all wisdom."

"That your way of saying I'm finally wizening up?"

"Maybe." She laughed. "Things are going well in group then?"

I nodded. "Absolutely. And there's this girl—"

"Ahh, now we come to it," she said, reclining back in her chair.

My face warmed, but in a pleasant—maybe even prideful—way. Not from embarrassment.

"This girl, she's nothing like anyone I've ever met. It's like I can't be anything but myself around her. For better and worse."

"Ernie, these all sound like a *good* things to my ears."

"I know, which is why I'm freaking out, I think. You might've noticed. I don't do so well with good things."

"As you probably know, Neyle has had some medical trouble this last year. He's been in physical therapy for a few months now, and the process is slow on the good days. But I recall the first thing his therapist told him. She said, 'This isn't going to hurt a bit. It's going to hurt like hell.'

"Hurting is part of that process. If you aren't hurting, you aren't pushing hard enough. Counseling is much the same. I believe what you're going through right now, the pain caused by your self-doubt, is a real sign that you're working at this. Call them growing pains."

I stood, feeling lighter, as though I'd sloughed off a few of the heavy rocks tied around my neck of late.

"Thank you."

A bemused smile broadened her face. "Need anything else?"

"Actually, I was also wondering if you'd come to some kind of official diagnosis for me."

Her eyebrows scrunched. "I plan to go over things again before our scheduled meeting next week, but I think my initial note was Major Depressive Disorder."

I smacked my leg. "Damn."

Dr. Laura's mouth widened. "Ernie, that's not a bad diagnosis. We can certainly work — "

I laughed. "I'm not upset. I had a bet with the group."

"And you lost." She smirked. "Abbey is very good."

It took another full week to get everything arranged for Baker's *project*. This was our first go, and I didn't want to screw things up. When the big day finally came, I was nervous but hopeful. We'd accounted for a lot of potential pitfalls — like weed, uncooperative roommates, and Baker's general lack of motivation. In short, this was game time.

"Baker, wake up." Luther shook him from his sleep for the fifth time. Unlike the four previous attempts, Baker stirred.

"Guh-way ... bro."

He pulled the blanket back over his head.

Luther gave me a concerned glance. I surveyed the room. Aside from a toppled stack of guitar magazines, the space was surprisingly tidy. Band posters dotted the walls. Books, movies, and video games shared a small bookcase. All things considered, a pretty typical college-guy space. Okay, there *were* two bongs being used as bookends, and the air smelled like a mix of pesticide and air freshener. I guess Baker had to make it his own somehow.

I picked up a glass of clear liquid off the bedside table and sniffed. *Definitely water.*

"Stand back."

Luther obeyed, and I flung the water on the ball of blankets and Baker.

"The-hell?"

Baker flew from the bed, struggling to free himself from the blankets. He stumbled and fell splayed-legged onto the floor. He looked up at us in his whitey-tighty underwear, nothing else.

"Thank God he's wearing something," Luther mumbled.

A pleasant surprise.

"Time for class," I said.

Baker glared with glassy, bloodshot eyes. "How'd you get in here?"

"One of your roommates let us in."

I didn't tell him that we'd also negotiated the removal of weed from the premises, at least the weed he knew about. That little bargain had cost Luther his favorite handheld video game system for a month. I knew he'd have more easily parted with an arm than let Baker's housemate use it, so I was really proud of the contribution.

"It's, like, four in the morning."

Luther yanked the strings on the blinds above the bed, flooding the room with light. "It's, like, eight-thirty ... loser."

Baker shielded his eyes with the back of his arm. "Bro, I don't have class until eleven."

"Says here..." I held up a piece of paper. "You've got sociology at ten."

"I don't have sociology until Monday."

I extend my hand to help him up. "Welcome to this week, Baker."

We got him to his ten o'clock. His eleven, too. At noon, I was to hand Baker over to Abbey, who would guide him to his lone afternoon class.

I joined them for lunch.

"So far, so good. Right, Bake?" I asked, not liking the ashen color his face had taken.

"I don't know, bro. My head kind of hurts."

Abbey patted his back. "Maybe eat something?"

Baker, clearly losing the irony of the girl with the eating disorder encouraging him to eat, said, "This is going to sound crazy … I'm not really all that hungry."

He looked as confused as I felt. Abbey's eyes widened.

I shrugged. *Damned if I knew how to coach someone through weed-withdrawal.* But if it couldn't be done with his stomach, I was sure we were headed for a long week.

Abbey snatched one of the fries off his plate and took the tiniest nibble possible. I could feel my jaw hanging open but was powerless to shut it. *Did she really eat a French fry?*

"They're good," Abbey said, covering her mouth with the back of her hand as if her body might reject the potato before it could reach her stomach.

Baker pushed one into his mouth, then another, while Abbey sipped her tea and I ate my tacos. As Abbey coached him through every other bite, I smiled.

When I came up with this idea, I wasn't sure we'd have enough in common to really pull together for each other. But I'd failed to recognize what we shared. We were all starving to feel worthwhile. Other people could probably find that worth inside them, but we needed to look outside to believe. We had to get a glimpse of ourselves being valuable to others. The idea was backwards, sort of like having to see the shadow to believe the object was real, but that's the way it was for us.

I was ashamed to think so, but I'd played team sports most of my life, and it wasn't until that moment I really understood why.

Day two with Baker didn't start as smoothly. Sing and I found him wide-awake, huddled in the corner, where the bed and the wall met. He was still dressed in the clothes he'd worn the day before.

"Hey, buddy. I brought breakfast." I dangled the greasy paper sack.

"It's terrible for you. You'll love it," Sing said, keeping her arms clamped around her torso.

She'd begged me not to make her go in the house but had relented when I told her how Abbey had tried the French fry. By comparison, anything we did to help Baker the rest of the week was trivial.

He didn't flinch. The area around his eyes was dark and hollowed out.

"Did you sleep last night, Bake?"

Finally, he moved, his head lolling listlessly from one side to the other. I sat on the edge of the bed. The movement must have jostled him enough to snap him from his thoughts.

"I'm freaking out, bro," he whispered.

His throat bobbed as he swallowed a few times. Sing left the room.

"What's up?" I asked.

He laughed hysterically. "The weed is gone, bro. All gone ... I checked everywhere. No one has any."

Sing returned with a glass of water. She wouldn't hand it to either of us directly, but placed it on the bedside table for me to give to Baker. He chugged half of the liquid down in a single gulp.

"I'm sure there's some left in the world somewhere," I said, patting him on the leg. "Let's get you cleaned up, fed, and off to class. Things'll look better after a hot shower."

He sat up, stiff and quick. "You don't understand. I smoke last thing before I go to sleep, and first thing when I wake up. I ... I can't handle this. It's like I'm thinking about everything all at once, and my brain won't slow down."

Sing inched toward the bed to stand next to me. "Do you have any medication for anxiety, Baker?"

"I never take it. Makes me feel funny."

"Baker." Sing's voice was stern, but she wasn't frowning. It was the first time I could remember seeing her address him without a scowl on her face. "Listen to me. You *can* do this. I spend every second of my day trying to control the world around me. Break things down into manageable bits. Would you try if I showed you?"

"I ... I don't know," he said.

Sing reached into the canvas messenger bag at her side. The sharp angles of her bobbed, purple-fringed hair barely shifted as she pulled out a small flip notebook. It was one of several, each a different color, including matching pens tucked in the spirals.

She opened the notebook to the first page. "What's the first thing you have to do this morning?"

He pulled at his hair. "Go to class?"

"No." Sing shook her head. "Think smaller."

"Get out of bed?"

"Good." She scribbled in the notebook. "Next."

"Shower."

"Smaller."

"This is hard." Baker scrunched his brow like he was trying to squeeze orange juice inside his skull. "Find something to wear?"

"Great. Next."

The list making went on until we'd mapped out his entire day, step by tiny step. Sing tossed Baker the notebook. He flipped through the pages, muttering the words as he read over them.

"This is awesome, bro."

Sing cleared her throat.

"Bro and Sing, I mean."

I flinched when she smiled.

"Ready to get started?" I offered him the sack of bacon, egg, and cheese burritos again.

He didn't take them.

"Breakfast isn't until page three."

Chapter Eighteen

Baker's week got easier as it progressed, and by Thursday, he met us at the front door of his house for the morning escort to class. I got him a jumbo-sized pack of gum. I'd read somewhere that it helped people quit smoking cigarettes, and to his credit, I rarely saw him not chomping on a piece. But he also informed me as soon as the week was up, he planned on getting so stoned he'd never remember the torment we'd put him through.

However, the little notebook Sing gave him was always in his pocket now. Baker consulted the pages before and after every class. So perhaps we'd made at least one lasting change in his behavior.

By two o'clock Friday afternoon, we'd accomplished our first group goal. Baker hadn't missed a single class all week. There really wasn't a big celebration or anything. Most of us had been forced to ditch a few classes to make sure Baker got to his, so there was a lot of catch-up reading and note-copying to be done.

For my part, I felt exhausted but pleased. I'd enjoyed hanging out with the group as much as doing something good for Baker. We weren't only becoming friends, we were partners now.

The afternoon was all but over by the time I drifted downstairs in the English building. The secretary was already gone for the weekend, so I moved quietly down the corridor of offices. Most of them were closed tight. A keyboard clicked from somewhere near the end of the hallway. A beam of light shone from the lone open door in that direction. I grinned.

I hadn't talked to Margery since the previous weekend—this time, more by accident. She'd left me a voice mail, and I'd left her one in return. Text messages confirmed we were both swamped. We'd seen each other in class, but I tried not to do much other than smile at her on those occasions. She'd smiled back, so I guessed we were still on good terms, even though I'd acted like a petulant jerk when I'd left her house.

I pushed the door open. "Still working?"

"Shit." Tea sloshed out of Margery's cup and onto the desk when she jumped. She threw a pencil at me, but I dodged it.

"Anyone ever tell you that you startle easily?"

She scowled. "Anyone ever tell you it's rude as hell to sneak up on people?"

"May I?" I pointed to the chair in front of her desk.

"Shut the door first."

I did as instructed and took my seat.

"So..."

She stretched her arms above her head. "So?"

"About last weekend—"

Margery stood. "You really don't need to apologize. I shouldn't have brought it up."

I raised my eyebrows. "What makes you think I was going to apologize?"

"Puh-lease. You read like an open book, Mr. Demps." She pointed at herself with her thumbs. "And books are kind of my job."

I laughed as she walked around the desk toward me. Her heels clicked on the hard floor as she passed by me. The sound of the door lock sliding into place drew my attention.

I glanced up as she put her hands on my shoulders from behind. She took her hair down, letting it fall gracefully to either side of her face. A slender finger rose to her mouth. My own mouth moistened in anticipation of what might be about to come.

I stood and slid the chair quietly out from between us. Her arms wrapped around my neck and pulled me nearer her. I grabbed her hips and lifted her off the ground an inch to meet me. Her body crumpled in my arms as I kissed her lips and down her neck, to trace along her exposed collarbone. My hands were on her legs, then on the insides of her thighs.

"You've..." She gasped. "Got *amazing* hands."

I spun her around so she leaned against the desk. My mind raced as I took in the curves of her body. *Where to go first?*

"I've always preferred to keep them busy."

I tugged my T-shirt off, pitching it on the floor while she undid the buttons of her blouse. My pants were already unbuckled and falling, and she pushed them the rest of the way to the floor to lay in a pile with her undergarments. Her fingers gripped my buttocks. Heat and pure lust swept over me as she pulled me between her legs. I raised her to sit on the desk.

Our bodies synchronized almost instantly. She yanked me closer with every thrust and rocked backward to allow our momentum to build. Every part of me screamed with the pleasure of the moment. But our mouths stayed locked, preventing us from crying out. Everything else moved for a singular purpose until the white-hot ecstasy we craved overcame us.

When we'd finished, I sat on the floor holding Margery's soft body close. Her skin was damp and cool against mine. We didn't speak, which was just as well. I had no words to describe the halo of pleasure and peace that had settled over me.

This was unexpected, essential, beautiful, and burning. *This* was nothing I'd ever experienced, and everything I ever wanted again. Right then, I was as whole as I'd ever been in my life. Margery had been the missing piece. A thought came to me so suddenly I laughed like it had been tickled out of me.

I'm falling in love with this girl.

Later that evening, after I left Margery alone to finish her grading, I decided to look Junkyard up. Maybe the leftover endorphins from my earlier encounter were filling me with a false sense of courage, but I finally felt ready to absorb whatever Junk would dish out. Or maybe, now that I had Margery and my new group counseling buddies in my corner, I wasn't as afraid of losing the fight with my only friend.

The familiar *tink* of the metal bat connecting with the ball echoed in the night air. Over and over again, the sound grew louder as I neared the batting cages. There were cheers, jeers, and laughter, too. I figured I'd find Junk at *Party Town*, the local amusement palace. It was his favorite place on the planet, and for good reason. Go-karts, video games, beer, pizza, alt rock music constantly blaring, free Wi-Fi—it was like a playground built especially for college students. I'd spent many Saturday nights there with the other guys on the team, showing off for the local ladies.

"You handle that stick like a girl, Junkyard," someone in the crowd shouted.

There was a violent *crack*. Junk took the cover off the ball. He could really hit when he was pissed. Which concerned me. If he was in a foul mood, the success of my mission might be in jeopardy.

"So's your mom," Junk said and a chorus of laughter followed.

I grinned, pushing through the onlookers to get up next to the chain link fence surrounding the cage.

"You've been working on your comebacks," I hollered.

His head jerked up, and a ball whizzed by. He shook his head in disgust. I wasn't sure if it was because of the missed ball or the sight of me. The machine hurled another, and he drove the ball into the nets at the back of the cage.

"Why don't you get in here and toss me a few for old time's sake?"

"I don't think that's a great idea, you not wearing a helmet and all," I said, knowing full-well Junk didn't give a shit about head protection when the balls were coming out at less than fifty miles-per-hour. "Besides, we'd be here all night waiting on you to hit one from me."

He pointed the bat in my direction. "Hear that, y'all? Mr. Star Pitcher is afraid to throw a few to the Dog."

He made a woofing sound.

"Come on, Ernie," someone near me said.

A hand clapped me on the shoulder, then another. They pushed me closer to the entrance to the cage, which worked out. Junk could hear me without having to shout now.

"I was actually hoping we could talk."

He showed his teeth in a half-smile, half-snarl. "Tell you what, if you can get three by me, we'll talk all you want."

"Fine," I said, knowing better than to argue.

Once Junk had issued a challenge, there was nothing to do but accept or be the source of locker-room jokes for all time. The crowd cheered when I slapped the red stop button on the control panel. The pitching machine chugged to a halt, and I entered the cage. I picked four balls out of the net behind Junk.

"You're going to need more than four."

"I don't think so."

I situated myself next to the machine. I stretched, working my arm in a circular motion to loosen the muscles. Not having pitched in weeks, I wouldn't be able to give him my *really* hard stuff. That was a formula for tearing something. But Junk had always had more trouble hitting the off-speed pitches, anyway.

I pulled my arm across my body and stared him down. He blew me a kiss. The onlookers cheered. They wanted a show, and I intended to oblige. I'd make the first pitch half-speed, a changeup.

The ball arched lazily, then dropped toward the plate. He swung and missed.

"Fuck," Junk shouted, tapping the end of his bat on the ground. "Give me a heater and we'll see how good those nets behind you can hold up."

I grabbed the next ball from the ground and went through my usual windup. Running my hands over the seams again was like cruising down the sidewalk on my bike with no training wheels. It was like swimming with no help for the first time and not drowning. The process was the most ordinary thing in the world, part of my nature, but I somehow needed to feel myself doing it to verify I was alive.

This time, I gave him the curve. Junk's eyes narrowed and his forearms tightened as the ball came at him up and in, right where he loved it. He unleashed his swing as the ball began to slide. He'd already made his decision and there'd be no recovery. The ball ended up below his knees over the outside of the plate, before bouncing off the ground and into the nets behind him.

I estimated the pitch to be one of the best curves I'd ever thrown. The crowd clapped as Junk cursed.

He leered. "That's going to cost you."

Assuming he wouldn't be expecting me to give him his favorite pitch on the third strike, I gave him the fastball he desired. A mistake. Junk lined the ball back at me. I ducked behind the pitching machine at my side as it whistled by. Another second and I'd have had my head split open. I could hear him laughing over the gasps of the onlookers.

So that's how he wants to play it, huh?

"I've got one left."

He choked up on the bat, moving his hands further up the neck to increase the control and force of his swing.

"Last shot to get that third strike, Hawk. Better make it count."

Oh, I will.

I unleashed my last pitch, another changeup, knowing I was going to bean him as soon as it left my hand. It wasn't hard enough to do any serious damage, but I sure hoped it would sting a little. I started walking toward the plate before I heard the thud and surprised murmuring.

Junk hopped up and down, shaking the arm I'd plunked, winced. "You little son of a bitch. You did that on purpose..."

I blew him a kiss this time.

Junk threw down his bat and charged. I put up my hands, sliding to the side as he lunged to catch him in a head lock. We fell to the ground to a chorus of, "Fight! Fight!"

He pulled a tuft of hair out of my arm so I'd let go. I did.

"That actually hurt, you big bastard," I said.

"Good, so does my arm."

"You were crowding the plate."

I grabbed ahold of his pec and twisted.

He yelped in pain then started laughing as we wrestled. Junk tried to snag my underwear for a wedgie. I fought him off, but soon we were lying on are backs with tears of laughter streaming from our eyes.

A thousand tiny bugs zoomed around the halogen lights above us.

"That has to be the first time in pitching machine history someone has charged the mound," I said, pushing to my feet.

I took his hand and helped him up.

"First time I've ever seen a curve that nasty in a batting cage. That's for sure." He gave me hard pat on the back. "You still got it, man."

"Haven't been away from the game that long."

Junk and I wandered to a picnic table he'd apparently claimed prior to his batting exercise. We climbed the bench, taking a seat on the tabletop. A metal bucket of iced down beers sat between us. He seized a bottle and knocked the cap off on the corner of the table.

He studied me. "Why'd you come out here tonight, Ernie? Pretty sure it wasn't to relive the glory days."

Maybe it was.

"I'm realizing some things. I need to apologize to you. Properly."

Junk growled, opening another beer. "Why'd you do it? Can you make me understand that at least?"

I pointed to his bottle. "You don't even offer me beer anymore—"

"You know you can have one—"

"No, that's not what I mean. You know me better than any other person alive. No bullshit. You've seen me throw a birthday cake across a room in a tantrum because I was so mad that my father didn't bother to call. I'm scared shitless that if I start drinking I'm going to be exactly like him. You get that."

I turned to him. "Remember when you sat with me while I stayed in bed crying for an entire week after mom died?"

He nodded. "Jesus, wasn't like I was going to leave you alone."

"It was more than that. You kept playing the same goddamned video game you'd already beaten a hundred times and offering me pizza like it was the cement that held the world together. It was like you thought if I could put a little pepperoni and sausage on my wounds, everything would be alright."

He scowled. "But you love pizza."

"I do." I sighed. "My point is, there are no secrets between us. If I knew why I was so fucked up, I'd tell you. You'd know — probably before I did. I couldn't help myself that day. Lots of days, in fact. I … I'm working on it."

I stared up at the sky so I wouldn't have to look at him anymore. High above the lights of the batting cages, the stars gleamed. My tears caused them to streak in my vision, making it seem as though they were all falling at once. Something I could relate to.

"I know, brother." Junk's beefy arm slid around my shoulder and squeezed. "I know."

Chapter Nineteen

"I'm nervous, Ernie." Abbey took two timid steps for every one of mine.

"Don't be. We're literally beside you all the way, right Sing?"

Sing glared, but the blindfold kept Abbey from seeing her frustration. We guided her down the greasy green-carpeted hallways of Frank's Pizza Palace until we stood in the middle of one of their party rooms. Long folding tables with steaming pizzas covering them lined the walls.

Abbey threw her head back and sniffed the air. "It smells amazing."

I put my finger to my mouth so the wait staff and friends who'd gathered wouldn't give anything away yet.

"Abbey, are you ready to complete your homework assignment?" I asked, using my best annoying-TV-host voice.

She nodded. Nervous excitement radiated off her like body heat.

"Let's get this over with before we have to hear her squeal." Sing tugged the blindfold off.

Abbey gasped as everyone cheered. She hugged Sing and moved into a circle of her friends we'd managed to round up for her.

Baker sauntered up. "We've got one of every kind of pizza offered by the best pie place in town. All for you, Abbey." She kissed his cheek, leaving him gaping.

I grabbed his hand for a shake and pulled him close. "Thanks for this."

"No worries, bro," he whispered. "One of my homies is a manger here. I tip him *really* well, if you get what I mean."

Abbey fanned tears as she walked from table to table inspecting the pizza. When she'd completed the circuit, she turned. She bit her lip, her face the color of ashes.

I stood next to her. "What is it?"

"I don't think I can do this. It looks delicious, and I really appreciate it. But if I eat any of this I don't know how I'm going to cope the rest of the week. This is really hard for —"

"We know. That's why you aren't going to do it alone."

I whistled and waved to Luther across the room. He crammed half a slice into his mouth before sliding a box out from under one of the tables. I grabbed Abbey's hand and pulled her along.

"Show her," I said.

Luther tugged a pink T-shirt from the box and held it over his chest. The words "Team Abbey" ballooned across the front. He handed her the shirt.

"We're going to wear them when we exercise with you this week."

"Exercise?" She glanced at me.

"Yep, we're going running with you every morning to help you work off the guilt from tonight's pizza splurge. What do you think?"

Her eyes were huge, blue, and hopeful. "I'd love that."

"There's this Emily Dickinson poem I read before almost every game. The opening lines are incredible. It goes —

Hope is the thing with feathers
That perches in the soul
And sings the tune without the words
And never stops — at all

As Luther handed out the shirts, I put my arm around Abbey. "We never stop hoping, right? Plus, this is for Luther, too. But I can't say how. Will you keep trying? For you and Luther, if nothing else?"

Her precisely tweezed brows scrunched, creating a look I'd call *Super-Determined Barbie*.

"Yes, I'll try. But you're going to tell me what it's about."

"I will. Promise. Now, let's get you some pizza."

The next morning, a slick of fog hovered over our school track, cutting the bleachers surrounding it in half. The footfalls of my fellow Team Abbey members sounded out an erratic rhythm behind me in the gloom. We'd found Abbey in surprisingly good spirits. I'd been worried, because even though she hadn't tried more than a bite of any one kind of pizza, she'd looked a little green by night's end.

We'd planned for such a problem, however. One of her friends had offered to sleepover with her. In fact, we'd arranged for someone to be with her every night of the week. Abbey was easily the most popular one amongst us, and it made helping her much easier. We had no shortage of people willing to pitch in.

This morning, as Abbey stretched and greeted the ten people who'd agreed to join us for our morning jog, I'd asked her friend for a report.

"She did alright. Well, I had to hide her phone so she wouldn't tally up the calories she'd taken in on her food calculator app. But other than that, it was pretty typical girl time."

I thanked her before she could elaborate on what "typical girl time" was.

I'd completed my third lap around the track when a familiar red head blurred by me. I sped up. "Margery."

She had headphones in and didn't hear me. I touched her arm. Her speed slowed as she turned. A smile brightened her face.

"Haven't bumped into you out here before," she said, jogging in place so I could come up beside her.

We set off at a slower pace so we could talk.

"Yeah, I'm out here with friends," I said.

Luther ran by and smacked me on the back of the head. "You better hurry. Don't want the guy with asthma to kick your ass."

Margery huffed out a breathless laugh. "I can see that. Nice shirts, by the way."

I'd forgotten about our pink outfits. "It's kind of a thing we're doing for counseling."

"Who's Abbey?" She gave me a sideways glance.

Her wry smile was more curious than jealous, but I thought I'd see if there was a button to be pushed nonetheless.

"You worried?"

"Only because there are fifteen people out here wearing them. She's got quite a fan club."

"She's actually great—"

As if on cue, Abbey jogged up beside us. "Thanks again for this, Ernie. You're a real sweetheart. See you at the finish line."

She sprinted ahead of us, the fog eventually blotting out her small frame.

"She's gorgeous," Margery said. Unlike her smile, there might have been a touch of jealousy in the tone of her remark.

I elbowed her gently. "*Now*, you're worried."

She shoved me. "No, *sweetheart*. Just making an observation."

I laughed. "She's in counseling with me. So was the guy who slapped me on the way by. Like I said, they're my friends."

"Doesn't seem like the normal jock crowd to me."

I jogged on a ways beside her in silence, concentrating on the sounds of my ragged breathing and heart thudding in my ears. I'd gotten out of shape in the few weeks since I'd left the team.

"They're not. Which is why I need them, I think." A stitch stabbed my side and I cursed under my breath. "And what if they aren't the normal jock crowd? You're not exactly the normal jock girlfriend."

Margery came to a sudden stop. It took me several paces to slow down enough to turn back.

I looked her over but didn't see any sign she'd been injured. "You okay?"

Her hands pressed to her thighs, and her green ear buds dangled limply over her shoulders. Tendrils of hair, damp with sweat and the moisture in the air, clung to her face. Her chest heaved visibly beneath a metallic-looking workout shirt.

Not wanting to get too cozy out in the open, I laid my hand on her shoulder. "Margery, are you alright?"

She nodded. "What did you say?"

I frowned, struggling to remember what I could have said to upset her so much. "I think I need them. They're my friends, and —"

"Not that, the other part." She moved her hand in a frustrated twirling motion.

"That you're not the usual jock girlfriend?"

She took off running again. *Oh shit.*

"Margery, wait." I caught up to her. "I'm sorry. I didn't mean to put you on the spot. It kind of slipped."

She was smiling again. *Thank God.*

"I'm your girlfriend, am I?"

We stopped. I ran my hand through my hair, which was getting longer and curlier by the day since I no longer had to trim it for the team. If I hadn't sweated out all of the moisture in my body before, I sure as hell had now. I licked my unbelievably dry lips. My heart thudded way too hard for the exercise to be the only culprit.

At last I said, "Yeah, I guess that's how I feel."

She punched me on the shoulder. "Good. Call me."

She sprinted off the track toward the parking lot. When I was sure she couldn't see or hear me, I whooped and punched the air. For the first time in my college career, I had a girlfriend. And it felt great.

Chapter Twenty

My group counseling mates and I sat in our circle chatting as we waited for Neyle. He'd had to cancel last week's meeting due to some kind of illness, but an e-mail had let us know this week's session was on. When he entered the room, he looked maybe a little more gray and fatigued than I'd seen him but otherwise okay. He maneuvered over to his jellybean jar, but after finding it empty, joined us in the circle.

"No candy tonight, I'm afraid." He unfolded the seat on his cane. "Apologies for last week, but I had a little setback."

"Are you okay?" Abbey tossed an unused cushion aside to make more room for him to get settled.

"I'm better. Just tired." Neyle sat and sighed. "Like all of you, I have good days and bad days. Speaking of, who wants to lead us off ton—"

"I'll go," Baker said.

Neyle flinched. "Oh ... okay."

"Good: I made it to every class last week. Week before, too."

Everyone but Neyle smiled. His mouth moved to speak, but he wasn't finding any words. At last he said, "Well, that's fantastic news, Baker. Really great. And the bad?"

Baker scrunched. "Nothing I guess."

He eyed Baker with suspicion. "Right. Abbey, what about you?"

"Good: I ate a lot of pizza."

Neyle gave a slow, grim nod, as if he were coaxing the horrible news that was sure to follow from Abbey's lips.

She smiled. "Bad: None."

"Okay, I give. What's up?" Neyle threw his hands into the air. "I'm gone a week and suddenly everyone figures out their problems? Ernie, Sing, Luther—I'm guessing you've had similar progress?"

Luther and I laughed. Sing covered a smile with the back of her hand.

Neyle grinned. "Fine. Keep your secrets, but we're going to celebrate." I glanced at Luther who only returned my curious look. "Get your things, we're getting ice cream. My treat."

The campus union was all but abandoned at eight o'clock at night, so we had our pick of tables. True to his word, Neyle got us all ice cream snacks from the freezer and a coffee for himself.

I chose a drumstick, a favorite from my childhood. Mom got me one after every game in little league. Taking a bite of the peanut-covered chocolate shell was like riding in a waffle cone-clad time machine. Sing picked out a rainbow-colored freeze pop, Abbey had a frozen yogurt cup, Luther had an orange sherbet pushup, and Baker munched on a double-decker ice cream sandwich of his own creation. We ate our treats, chatted, and did everything *but* discuss our problems.

As everyone left, Neyle caught me by the sleeve. "Ernie, can I have a second?"

"Sure."

He studied me from behind a set of bifocals, his eyes reflecting the cafeteria lights. "You had something to do with all this, didn't you?"

"Not sure what you're talking about."

His laugh echoed in the high ceilings of the room.

"Sure you don't. Listen, whatever it is you're doing with this group, keep it up. They're changing—*you* are changing. All for the better, I might add. And as much as I'd like to take credit for this when Laura asks, I can't."

I patted his shoulder. "You're the reason we're here, last time I checked. I show up."

He smiled with only half of his face, creating a thoughtful—or maybe amused—look combined with his bushy mustache. "Well, we are certainly glad you showed up."

I stood a little straighter and felt a little taller. In all the years I'd played baseball, I'd never been named a team captain or asked to lead—for fairly obvious reasons. The idea of inspiring others had always terrified me, because it was another load of expectations I didn't want to carry around. But this was different. I found myself craving the challenge of sharing the burdens of the group, and leading them however far we could manage to go together.

"Can I ask a favor?"

Neyle leaned back on his heels. "You can certainly ask."

"It's about the group — Luther specifically."

I explained what we'd been up to, and laid out my plan for helping Luther. The only small detail I hadn't worked out was how to get his dad front and center for the show. I figured Neyle might be willing to help.

"So that's it. You've decided to band together to work on your problems?"

I nodded.

"Well, I suppose that is the point of group counseling. But I'm not sure about this thing with Luther, Ernie. Have you met his father?"

"No."

"I see." His gaze swept over me. "And you think this is a good idea? The others are on board as well?"

"I do. They are."

"Well, there are a lot of confidentiality issues we have to be careful of." His words were doubtful, but the mischievous grin on his face said he loved the idea.

"Please. I have to get him on campus. Couldn't you pull some strings? Tell him you need to meet about Luther's grades. Anything."

Neyle scratched at his cheek. "Luther's mother knows he's in counseling. Maybe I could work through her."

I put my hands on his shoulders. "Will you try?"

"I will, but it might not work."

"Fair enough."

I gave him my cell number so he could let me know one way or the other.

Neyle set off in the opposite direction as me, his cane tapping out his steps before he took them. "Goodnight, Ernie."

"Goodnight," I shouted back.

As I left the student union, I was greeted by a throng of stars overhead. I blew out a heavy breath and lolled my head back to take them in. The swelling pride that had filled me earlier had seemingly dissipated into the ether as soon as I'd stepped outside. I still felt more important than I'd ever been in my life but, somehow, also very small.

I didn't have a good reason to sit outside the Field House at nearly midnight. My feet led me there while my mind was busy doing everything but caring where I ended up. Logically, my dorm *was* in the general direction. But if logic were a motive, why I hadn't I gone inside and to bed? Hell if I knew, but there I was, stretched out on one of the cool concrete benches and counting stars like it was my job.

"What's a bad *hombre* like you doing out this late without a pretty girl by his side?"

I lifted my head to see Coach Ramirez standing near my feet, hands on the waistline of his tracksuit. He swatted my legs so I'd make room for him to sit. I did and smiled.

"Coach." I squeezed his hand when he offered it.

"How's life, *muchacho*?"

I mulled his words. This man deserved an honest answer from me, as I was pretty sure he'd saved my life, or at least made me live it, by getting me into counseling. So I searched deep inside my head, heart, or wherever the place was I locked away things like regret, love, and truth. I was certain they were all cellmates in the same tiny box.

"I'm great. Really great."

"And to think I was afraid you'd dropped out." He laughed his piercing bray of a laugh. If the campus snoozed, it wouldn't be for much longer.

"The counseling, it's working out?"

I nodded. "Neyle and Laura are awesome. Made some from friends, too."

"Imagine that. Our brooding Ernie making friends who don't play baseball — not sure if your old coach approves of that by the way. Next you're going to tell me you've found a girl."

He winked and threw his arm around my shoulders. *The son of bitch knew.* Had I blushed?

"You *did* find a girl. That's great. Anyone I know?"

That was one truth I couldn't share with him for obvious reasons. He'd think I was out of my mind for dating the Walrus's daughter. Hell, I thought I was out of my mind for dating her.

"I really can't say—"

Coach Ramirez held up his hand. "It's a secret. I can respect that. Is she pretty?" He waggled his eyebrows suggestively.

I laughed out loud along with him this time.

He checked his watch. "*Aye mio!* My pretty girl is going to send out the attorneys if I don't get home soon. But I'm glad I bumped into you."

"Why's that?" I stood with him.

"I've gotten calls from a couple of buddies in the minors asking about you." He hugged me around the neck. "They wanted to know if you were still committed to college. Said they'd make a spot for you whenever you wanted to give pro ball a run."

"Coach, I'm not—"

"I know, I know. Seems like you're getting things figured out. But this hasn't been the easiest semester for you, and…" He stuck his hands in the pockets of his jacket and stared at the ground. Something was up. Coach Ramirez typically sought eye contact like he was mining for gold.

I frowned. "What is it?"

"Coach Price still isn't sold on you coming back to the team next semester. I've tried with him. There's still a chance, but I can't make any promises."

It was my turn to put my arm around him. "Coach, I'm not sure what I want to do right now. But whatever happens, I'm cool with it."

An uncomfortable knot in my stomach protested my words. The sensation set off an avalanche of doubts in my mind. If I wasn't playing baseball, I wasn't on scholarship — if I wasn't on scholarship, I wasn't sure I could afford school — if I wasn't at school, would Margery and I continue to exist? By the end of the chain of thoughts, I was buried and suffocating.

Then the voice came. Its words freezing me with truth: *Wasn't this what you wanted? You can let your mother down, and it won't even be your fault.*

"Ernie, did you hear what I said?"

I blinked heavily trying to clear my head. "Sorry, what?"

"I said, if you want to look into the pro ball offers, stop by my office. We can talk through your options. I'll help you get wherever you want to go, you know that."

I nodded. But I was getting the feeling that maybe I didn't need a guide in life so much as I needed a guardian angel. Coach Ramirez was a good man, but I'd never seen wings sprout from his back.

Chapter Twenty-One

After my talk with Coach, sleep was never going to be an option. So, as a dude rite of passage, I decided to make my first random, midnight text to my new girlfriend.

You awake?

She answered almost immediately.

I know you're not drunk ... Is this a booty text, Mr. Demps?

She included a smiley face, so I knew she wasn't too annoyed.

NO ... well, maybe. Ever ridden on a motorcycle at 1 AM?

Can't say that I have. Is this an official offer?

Yes. I'll send over the paperwork.

I'd barely mounted my bike when she replied.

Give me 10 minutes. And don't judge me without my makeup on.

Don't judge ME for being the guy who shows up at your house at 1 AM.

Deal.

I hopped on my motorcycle and sped across town. My high school baseball coach had once told me, "Demps, nothing good happens after midnight, so keep your ass in bed." Did it count if I never actually made it to bed?

I knocked on Margery's door and hoped not. She answered quickly, not looking particularly dreary-eyed.

"I'm sorry. Did I wake you with my text?" I asked.

She groaned. "Unfortunately, no. I've been working on a paper and watching Vampire Diaries reruns. Okay, mostly watching Vampire Diaries reruns."

"You're into vampires, huh?"

"I'm more into the hot, ultra-broody guys who play vampires on TV. Don't judge."

I pulled her into my arms. "I can be ultra-broody. And I'm right here."

"Don't think I haven't noticed." She laughed. "Where we headed?"

"Anywhere." I grinned down at her. "Everywhere."

She stretched to kiss the underside of my chin. "Sounds like my kind of perfect."

We ended up at the municipal gulf course located in a park, at the edge of city limits. I'd idled my motorcycle along the cart path with the lights off until we found the perfect spot. Small town, few cops, had its advantages. Now, Margery's head rested on my chest as we lay beneath the stars on the green of the seventh hole.

"What's eating you?" Margery ran her fingers over my stomach, tickling me enough to tense the muscles beneath my shirt.

"What isn't?"

"That bad?" She stroked my face with the back of her hand.

The touch was equal parts calming to my brain and exciting to my body. Her skin smelled of lavender, probably from body lotion. The odor mingled pleasantly with the scents of cut grass and lilac blossoms playing in the night air. I took her hand and kissed each of her fingers.

"Not any more." I rolled on top of her, straddling her legs and letting the weight of my body rest on my elbows.

She stared at me as I brushed the hair away from her face. Her eyes were wide and fragile, like a green pond slicked with a thin layer of ice. My insides mimicked her look. There was an incredible beauty in how I felt about Margery, but also the vulnerability of frolicking around on something pristine and delicate. Any sudden moves and the whole thing might give out from under us. But damned if I didn't think the plunge would be worth it.

I kissed her.

"What is this?" she asked in between gasps for air.

I forced myself free of her searching hands and mouth long enough to tug my shirt off. The humidity from the recent rains had taken the chill out of the air, hinting at the hot summer nights that would soon come. A different kind of warmth surged through my body.

"Other than a hell of a lot of fun?" I unbuttoned her jeans.

"Not just that." She placed her hand behind my neck and drew me back to her. "I'm talking about you..." Her lips moistened with a flick of her tongue. "Me..." She untangled her legs from mine and wrapped them around my waist. "Us."

I slid my hands under her sweatshirt and caressed her soft flesh. Her moans sent my pulse racing.

"To quote Wordsworth, 'The music in my heart I bore, long after it was heard no more.'"

She gave a breathless laugh and helped me push my jeans lower. "Which means?"

"It means..." She'd wiggled her own pants down to her ankles, so I pulled them the rest of the way off along with her panties. I tossed them onto a pile of clothes we'd started on the damp grass next to us. The heat of her body melded with mine as I slipped back between the silkiness of her legs. "That no matter what this is it will always be a part of us. And me."

"I think." She bit my neck as I entered her. "I can live with that."

The next evening, I decided to ask Margery out for our first dinner date. She had asked me what *this*, our relationship, was. The simple question had stirred me more than the moment had allowed me to realize.

My time spent away from her was becoming increasingly uncomfortable, and my time with her more essential. I'd never experienced what it meant to have someone be an actual piece of who I was, but I was beginning to understand the concept. When I parted from her, a gaping black hole was left in my thoughts, drawing everything else in my head back to where she'd been. I stared at my dorm ceiling thinking about her, wondering if she was thinking about me. If I dwelled on what our next touch would lead to for too long, my stomach twirled. She'd become a source of beautiful misery in my life that only her presence could sooth. I think philosophers called it a paradox. What they hell did they know about college romance? What did I, for that matter? I wasn't sure if I'd written the script, or was simply reading from it.

Margery had been somewhat reluctant about cavorting with me in public, so I chose a spot far away from campus for our meal. I couldn't see any real chance of us being spotted nearly a county away.

The dive diner glowed like a filth-covered yard light from its spot along one of the many rural roads extending from our little college town. We'd driven by a dozen cornfields on our way to the grease-coated hideaway. I couldn't honestly even remember how I'd learned about the place. Probably passed by it on one of my many motorcycle explorations.

Margery smirked at me from over the top of her menu. "Sign out front said it's the world's best apple pie, so we've got that going for us."

"Let's hope it comes with a side of hand sanitizer." I blotted up some syrup left on our table with a paper napkin. "The price of privacy, right?"

I touched her knee under the table, enjoying the way

her cool skin warmed beneath my fingers. Being together out in the open felt good on the inside, too. It was a pinch during an amazing dream. This was definitely real.

Margery smiled. She put her menu down and slid her hand beneath the table. "Oh God, I touched something squishy. It wasn't you."

We yanked our arms back in mutual disgust and laughed. After placing our order with an appropriately disgruntled waitress, we sipped our iced tea and talked.

"You seem a little ... off. Everything okay?" she asked.

Margery's glasses had slipped halfway down her nose, making her more teacher-like than she'd probably want me to mention. So I didn't.

A panicked flutter filled my chest. "I guess."

My indifference was only skin deep. I felt something was happening between us, something beyond lust for my part, but was the timing right for me to say so? Did she feel the same way? Furthermore, what was she going to think about my talk with Coach? I couldn't very well confess my growing feelings for her and then say I might be moving across the country to play professional baseball.

I took too big of a drink of my tea and sputtered into my napkin.

She frowned. "Well, *I guess* you'd better tell me about it."

Unless I intended to satisfy my curiosity of seeing what kinds of monsters hid in this dump's bathroom, I had no place to run. So I told her about my talk with Coach. Margery listened patiently, but her chin crept higher and higher as I spoke, as if she were bracing for a blow.

When I finished, she smoothed her napkin on her lap. "That's a big opportunity, what are you going to do?"

Nothing without you, my brain screamed.

But that seemed a little too bold for this stage in our relationship, so I went with, "I'm not sure."

"Can you go to school and play pro ball in the summer?"

"Not sure about that, either," I said. "But I know it would be the end of my college baseball days. The NCAA won't let me play once I start getting paid. I'm not even positive about how much money I'd make. The minors don't pay a lot, so I might not be able to cover tuition. And the team might not want me to do both."

She bit her lip. "Hadn't thought about all of that."

"Margery, I need to know something."

"Yes?" Her voice was high, her eyes wide, and her mouth a grim line. She was preparing herself for anything I might say next, I was sure of it.

I gnawed my cheek until courage, or stupidity, tipped the scales enough for me to speak. "I know you don't like baseball. But if that was my life—I mean my entire life—could you, would you still want to be a part of it? I guess I'm asking, is there a chance for this to actually go somewhere, or are we joy riding?"

The words were heavy, and yet, they somehow managed to float in the air between us an impossibly long time. I closed my eyes and counted seconds waiting for an answer. *One one-thousand. Two one-thousand. Three one-*

thousand. Four one —

"Ernie."

My neck stiffened as I looked up at her. I'd been rehearsing a lie in my head to lessen the blow, so I said it out loud. "If you want to keep this casual, I get it."

"Shush." Her cheeks reddened and she leaned over the table. "I'm ready to explore *us*. Let's see where this goes. Together."

"Burger?" The waitress banged a plate down in front of me.

Margery took her grilled cheese.

We ate mostly in silence, exchanging shy smiles and nervous laughs. I took her hands in mine as we waited on our check, but we still didn't talk much. The hot flash of whatever we'd had initially had become a steady flame. But it was as if we both knew words might still be able to puff it out if we uttered them.

We exited the diner to a chorus of chirping crickets. When we rounded the corner to where Margery's car was parked, I pulled her close to me. Our hands came together, then our mouths, and at last our bodies.

"If it isn't Psycho E himself."

My jaw went rigid mid-kiss. Margery pulled away from me slowly, but stayed at my side. David Goldstein, the King Asshole, led a group across the gravel parking lot in our direction. Bash was with them, but I didn't recognize the others.

"Fuck," I muttered. "Play it cool. Maybe he won't recognize you."

Margery partially hid behind me.

David came to stop a couple feet away from us. His crew fanned out behind him. It was a mix of girls and guys, most of whom were busy talking amongst themselves and not paying attention to us.

Bash brushed by David. He wasn't smiling. "What's up, Hawk?"

"Grabbing a bite." I bumped his fist when he offered it. "You guys?"

"The pie," David said with a wink. He nodded over his shoulder at two of the girls behind him.

Bash grimaced. "Same." He regarded Margery only for a moment, but I was certain I saw his eyes bulge slightly.

I would have given anything to pull him aside and beg him not to say anything if he recognized her, but that would have only drawn more attention to us.

"We better get going," I said. "Good seeing you."

Margery moved out from behind me.

David grabbed my arm. "Somebody is hot for teacher. What's up, Ms. Price?"

Fuck. I wiped my palms on my jeans to remove the sweat. Margery's face tightened. She gave a curt waive and slid into her car.

"That's coach's daughter," David said.

"I realize that." I shook free of his grasp.

Bash's face wrinkled like he'd been slapped. "What are you thinking, Ernie?"

"We gotta go." I turned toward the car.

"Hold on a second. We need to talk." David grabbed my arm. *Again.*

Heat washed over me in waves. I spun on him. "I don't have anything to say to you. Enjoy your pie."

"I think you do. You owe us an explanation for why you screwed us over. Are you crazy, or just a chicken shit?" He poked me in the chest, and someone in the group behind him gasped.

A buzzing sound filled my ears and my vision clouded. All I could see was his stupid face, and it pissed me off all that much more.

"Get in the car, Ernie," Margery said, but her voice was only a whisper in the back my mind.

I stepped close to David. "I've explained myself to everyone I care about. I'm not surprised you were left off the list. And if you touch me again, I'm going to break your nose, you fuck."

"Get in the car."

David stuck his dimpled chin out. "You better listen to your girlfriend, traitor."

He was right. I needed to leave. Fast. I turned—

"Don't think screwing the coach's daughter is going to get you back on the team."

The ringing in my ears turned into a blaring siren of rage. I twisted as David unleashed a punch. His fist narrowly missed my head as I ducked to one side. Before he could recover, I buried my fist in his belly. He doubled over, gasping for air. I shoved him to the ground with the toe of my shoe.

Bash stepped in between us with his fists clinched, but he looked more hurt than angry. "What the hell is wrong with you?"

I backed away slowly.

"Get in the goddamned car, Ernie!"

That time, I did.

Chapter Twenty-Two

"Holy shit, holy shit, holy shit..." Margery said as we cruised down one country road after another. And I thought the expression summed things up fairly succinctly. We were most definitely in righteous and immaculate excrement without the hope of a prayer.

"Did you have to hit him?" The high whine of the engine and her voice mingling in unfortunate harmony.

"Yes."

"Why?"

"Why do you think? Because he's such a swell guy?"

She went quiet.

"I'm sorry. This isn't your fault. He and I go back a ways. You got in between two objects that have been destined to collide for a long time."

"No." She slapped the steering wheel. "Us going out to dinner was a silly risk. I knew better."

"I chose the spot." I banged my head against the seat with sudden realization. How could I have been so stupid? "I'm so sorry."

"What for?"

"I remember how I knew about the place. A bunch of us from the team went there after a game my freshman year. I think some of the guys drive out here a lot." I tugged at my hair. "I did this."

She patted my arm. "Don't be ridiculous. You couldn't have known they'd pick today to come back."

I had a knack for pushing the eject button when things were going good in my life. Had I known, somewhere deep down, that there was a chance we'd get caught? I stomped the floorboard.

Margery glanced over at me. "I refuse to let you take all the blame for this. Since I met you, I haven't been able to think straight. It's like I'm not getting enough oxygen to my brain, so my heart—and other things—have been doing all the thinking."

One of her hands rested on the gearshift between us. I took it in mine. "Same here. But it feels right—"

"I know," she said. "That's why I'm so conflicted. If this is as good as I think it is, why are we hiding? Why do I feel like this needs to be kept a secret?"

I sighed. "You know why. Your goals are important to you. Not screwing them up is important to *me*."

I let go of her hand so she could steer us into her driveway. But there was something else behind the breaking our touch. Why *had* I punched David? He'd been a prick so many times before, I'd pretty much given him the douchebag discount. I was a pitcher, and a damn good one most days. I knew how to control my emotions during stressful situations. Somewhere deep down I'd decided not to this time.

"Maybe it's best for us to lay low for a while," Margery said.

My chest tightened, but too late to keep her words from burrowing into my heart. Laying low sounded a lot like staying away from each other to my ears. She was right. I nodded.

"Are you mad at me?"

I'm mad at me. And I'd have liked nothing more than to punish myself for it. I shook my head as much to answer as to drive the darkness from my mind.

"Say something."

Could she handle what I was really thinking? That, somehow, I was sabotaging our relationship without even knowing it. No, she wasn't ready to hear that any more than I was ready to utter it.

I kissed her cheek. "It's going to be okay. David is probably embarrassed. He won't tell anyone if he doesn't have to. Bash is a friend. We'll talk, and I'll make him understand. Until then, we'll keep it quiet between us—just until the semester ends."

"Until the semester ends." Her lips parted with a sigh. I missed kissing them already. "That's only a few weeks, right?"

I opened the door. "Right."

My life continued on without Margery being a regular part of it. Each day I'd get up, text her good morning, get dressed, and go to class. At the end of the day, I'd come back to the dorms, eat, shower, and text her good night. What choice did I have? I'd stepped in a big pile of shit. I knew it. Margery knew it. I was certain David knew it. The question was when would it start to stink?

We were at the mercy of one of the biggest jerks on the planet, and punching him in the gut wasn't going to win me any allowances. We could call and text, but otherwise, we'd try stay out of each other's paths.

I'd successfully repeated the routine all the way through to Friday. One week down, and the same horrible pit of worry filled my stomach. The other boot was going to drop, and no matter how far I ran, I wasn't sure if I could ever get out from under it. The three weeks left in the semester might as well have been a lifetime.

Now, as I picked my way through my cafeteria mystery casserole, Luther's dusky brown eyes swept over me for what felt like the hundredth time. He was doing his best to make me come clean, but there wasn't much left to confess.

"Dude, are you going to tell me what's up?"

I pulled a well-gnawed pencil out of my mouth. "What?"

Luther sighed. "You're in the clouds. Is it the girl?"

I waved my hand dismissively.

"Yep, definitely the girl." Luther crossed his arms. "If you need to talk—"

"I'm good. Where are we at with Sing again?"

"Fine." Luther tapped his phone. "Baker is on the snacks. I've combed her social media sites and picked out some of her favorite movies and music."

"Great, now we just have to get into her room and stay there ... that came out way more inappropriately than I'd imagined."

Luther laughed. "Abbey is in Sing's dorm. Said most of the girls who work the front desk are her sorority sisters. As long as we aren't too rambunctious, she can get them to look the other way when it comes to curfew checks."

"Perfect. And I'm still going to be the first to show?"

Luther nodded. "God help you if she's in a bad mood."

"I'll be fine. I'll run."

"Or maybe take that pepper spray they use on bears," Luther said.

I checked my watch. "I've got to get to class, but I'll see you tonight."

At half-passed eight, I knocked on Sing's door. There was the standard issue dorm room corkboard on the front. Unlike most of the others I'd passed on the way to her room, Sing's wasn't ornately decorated. There were six curling ribbons tacked up: red, green, yellow, white, black, and blue. That was it.

"Pizza guy," I shouted when she didn't immediately answer.

Several curious heads poked out down the hallway. A couple of the girls quickly disappeared when I waved, but one of them took the time to ask what kind of pizza I was holding.

She also withdrew when I told her I couldn't go to her room and share.

"I didn't order pizza," Sing's muffled voice came from the other side of the door. "And you're supposed to leave it at the front desk. I'll call campus security."

That failed spectacularly. *Might as well swing for the fences.*

"Sing, it's Ernie. Can I come in?"

The door swung open. Sing wore one of those animal beanie hats with the long ears—a rabbit. Her fleece pajamas also had rabbits on them. She clutched a pillow in the shape of a rabbit head to her body.

She squinted sleepily at me. "What are you doing here?"

"Somebody loves rabbits." I smiled. "Were you asleep already? It's Friday night."

She glowered. "My parents call me at 2;30 a.m. every Saturday morning—4:30 in the afternoon Taiwan time. So I go to sleep early."

"That sucks. Can't they call you later?"

"No. That would interfere with family dinner. And that's when my father wants to call, presumably to make sure I'm in bed early on a Friday night." She rolled her eyes. "Can I go back to sleep now?"

I held up the pizza box. "I was in the neighborhood. Thought you might want to share."

If there was such a thing as a skeptical stance, Sing adjusted herself into it.

"You were in my dorm, wandering around, and thought I'd want pizza? Ernie, we've barely talked outside of group. Don't jack with me."

Luther was right, I should've brought the pepper spray.

"Okay, I confess. I needed someone to talk to and no one else would answer their phones. Can I come in?" I stuck my lip out in a mock-pout. "Please?"

She stepped aside with an audible grumble.

I placed the pizza box on her desk, which was tidy and clear. She immediately picked it up and placed a folded towel beneath. The entire room was impeccable. A small rug was placed symmetrically in front of her sink. A laptop lay on her bedside table along with a tiny picture frame of what I assumed to be her family. The only sign that a college student actually lived there was her bed. One side of the covers had been turned back. There was a Sing-sized imprint on it.

"Mind if I pop a squat?" I pulled out her desk chair, noting how she squirmed when I touched it.

Three more people were about to cram in here. *This would get interesting, fast.*

She nodded and sat on the bed with her legs crossed under her.

I needed to stall.

"How was your week?"

"Cool, I guess." Sing rubbed her eyes. "No offense, Ernie, but I really don't like guests. And I need to sleep. Sooo…"

"I'm having girl problems," I blurted.

"And you came to me?"

"Sure." I opened the pizza box and pretended to inspect the contents. "Why not?"

She sighed. "Fine. Tell me *all* about it. I'm *so* interested. But you better wash your hands before you touch that pie if you expect me to share it with you."

"You're really trying hard, aren't you?" I grinned.

She shrugged. "Guess making friends hasn't really ever felt as important to me as it has lately."

"*That* I can relate to," I said.

For reasons I couldn't guess, other than the sake of wasting time until the others showed up, I told Sing everything. From my baseball indiscretions, to getting involved with Margery, and finally about my staying-in-school conundrum—I let her have it. And she listened, never interrupting and never nodding off.

When I finished, she walked quietly over to her tiny dorm closet. There were several cubbies with letters on the front.

"You alphabetized your closet?"

She looked over her shoulder. "You don't?"

"No."

She turned to me, smiling. *She was screwing with me.*

"Someone loves rabbits *and* has a sense of humor," I said.

She handed me a wad of napkins. I knew better than to touch her piece of pizza, so I offered the box and she selected one. After she rearranged the toppings to what I assumed was a more pleasing pattern, she sat on the floor with her back against the bed.

We munched without saying anything until I asked, "So, what do you think? Am I screwed?"

She held up a finger while she finished chewing and then swallowed. It wouldn't have surprised me if she counted every bite.

"You're definitely screwed—"

"Thanks for the pep talk." I chuckled.

"You didn't let me finish. You're screwed, but not because of why you think."

I stretched my legs. "Do tell."

"Have you ever heard of the psychological primary colors? The idea is six primary colors—red, green, blue, yellow, white, and black—are dominant because all other colors can be described using some combination of those. We're talking thousands of possible colors, and all of them come from only six. I think it's an empowering concept. You've noticed I struggle with order?"

I rubbed my chin. "Thinking disorder might be more of your problem, but okay."

"Ha, ha. You know what I mean … The world is too big for me, Ernie. It's like I have a thousand problems going through my brain every second with millions of possible answers. So I try to make things smaller by controlling, well, everything. At least that's what Dr. Laura tells me. I use those colors as a reminder that almost every problem can be resolved with a few simple answers."

Finally! The markers, ribbons—all of it—made so much more sense.

"Mind sharing those with me?"

"I think they're different for all of us." Sing cocked her head. "Which is also why I think you're screwed. In our own lives, we're the colors all the rest come from. You aren't anyone else's creation. You do the creating. Get angry at the world if you want, but your problems are of your own making. I don't think you've figured that out yet."

While it was never fun to hear everything was your fault, I had no real argument. More than that, I was beginning to see Sing and I had a bond. We were yin and yang on the psychosis spectrum. She channeled most of her anger and frustration outward, and I directed mine inward. But the result was the same. We were looking for answers in all the wrong places.

I smiled. "I'd give you a hug if I thought you wouldn't punch me in one of my favorite parts."

"Oh, I totally would." She returned my grin. "Wanna know the real bitch about all that color stuff?"

"Sure."

"I'm color blind."

I was laughing so hard I barely heard the knock on the door.

"Sounds like you two are having a good time," Abbey said, pushing by me.

She was in her pajamas also, but unlike Sing's rabbit-clad offering, Abbey's were silk and classy.

"Ernie, would you fetch Baker?"

I ducked into the hall and found him chatting up the girl three doors down. I cleared my throat to get his attention.

"Call me, bro," he said, handing the girl a bag of chips.

"Get in here."

I flipped his ponytail when he entered. Sing had crawled to the back corner of her bed. Her knees were clasped to her chest, and her eyes darted around like a trapped, wild animal.

"What's going on? Why is Baker in my room? Why would Baker *ever* be in my room?"

Baker opened his mouth to speak.

Abbey jumped in front of him. She held her hands up like Sing had a gun leveled at her. "We thought—you know for your group project—a slumber party might do you some good."

"You've all lost your minds. What about the curfew? What about the mess? What about—"

"We've covered it," I said. "All of it. You just need to sit here and chat, maybe even watch a few movies. Think you could do that?"

"What movies? I don't see any of you with movies. Baker, if you drop a single chip, I'll stab you with something dull and filthy."

Baker crammed another handful of cheesy chips into his mouth and giggled. There was another knock.

Sing jumped. "Oh God. Now what?"

I let Luther in.

"No, no. Absolutely not," Sing said. "There's not enough space in here. You're *completely* obliterating the fire code."

Luther held up a plastic movie case and waggled it seductively. "I brought Kill Bill."

Sing's eyes narrowed. "One or two?"

Luther fished into his book bag. "Both."

Clearly defeated, her shoulders slumped. "Okay, we can try this. But only Abbey is allowed to touch my bed. Boys on the floor. Shoes on at all times."

Baker groaned.

"When my parents call, it's silence or death. You choose." Sing pointed at each of us.

"Deal." I put my arms around Baker and Luther. "Who wants pizza?"

Chapter Twenty-Three

The worst part about being away from Margery was not being able to touch her. I missed the feel of her skin in my hands. Her smells hounded me. If I caught a whiff of her perfume or shampoo on another girl, I'd have vivid flashbacks to the nights we'd spent together. It was like I had lover's PTSD.

Class with her was particularly cruel. I could see her and hear her, but touching was a child's dream of touching a wisp of cloud. I sat in my usual seat in the back corner, staring at the ground far below the window or reading poetry. They were the only things keeping my mind off of the exquisite torture I was being put through.

The one positive was that David had stopped coming to class. Margery texted me one afternoon saying she'd been notified he'd dropped the course. I'm sure the ass figured she'd fail him anyway, but I knew Margery well enough to know she would have given him a fair go.

Does that mean I can see you? I'd texted.

Not yet. Be patient.

What about now?

No.

Damn!

You're a poet. What's all that stuff about absence strengthening the heart's fondness?

LIES … Damn. Dirty. LIES.

Ultimately, I knew she was right. A few weeks of real discretion on our part, and the storm would likely pass. But damn was it hard to see beyond the gray clouds hovering over us at the moment.

Still. I had bigger things to chew on, like planning Luther's big day. I had to figure out a way to clue him in so he'd be prepared, but not give away the entire plan. If Luther knew all the details, he might not be able to go through with it. He'd never said as much directly, but he was terrified of his father. I knew a little something about fearing a parent, and the way Luther's eyes glazed and his voice changed when he talked about him told me all I needed to know.

So I'd carefully laid out the scheme. My buddy Big would put him through a regular Army PT routine and we'd record it on video to show his dad. We'd do push-ups, sit-ups, and running—the works. He'd told me the sit-ups and run, so long as he could take a couple of hits on his inhaler first, wouldn't be an issue. The push-ups, however, were a weak point. So I'd started training with him. Every day for three weeks, we went through the same routine. Sit-ups, push-ups, and run … Sit-ups, push-ups, and run … Sit-ups, push-ups, and run.

Abbey and Sing joined us for most of the runs, a habit we'd started for Abbey's project and never stopped. Baker did the workouts with us, when it didn't interfere with his band practice. He was surprisingly strong and could knock out the push-ups faster than I could. The running was mostly beyond him, however. He could chug the first mile out, but he'd end up wheezing and coughing by the fifth lap. We all deduced the reason.

By the time we reached the morning of his showcase, Luther was acing the physical stuff. Now, it was simply a question of mental preparedness.

"You ready for this?" I asked as we made the short walk from our dorms to the track.

Luther gave a grim nod. He wore short shorts and knee-length socks.

"Who dressed you this morning, Dr. J?" I asked, trying to lighten his mood.

"What?"

"Nothing." I stopped in front of him. "You've got this. There's nothing in the routine you can't do. Big is a gruff dude, but he's cool. He'll probably scream at us a lot, though."

"It's not that. I know it's not going to make any difference. Dad won't think differently of me because of some stupid workout video."

Luther stared blankly into the distance. *Fear.* I recalled Neyle's skepticism the night I'd asked him to help with the plan. This could still go six-shades of south.

"Have I ever shown you my tattoos?"

"No." He smirked. "Can't say that you have."

I pulled my shirt off and turned my back to him.

"Those are impressive feathers, but I don't see—"

"Take a closer look," I said. He took a cautious step forward. "There are seven of them."

"Why seven?" he asked.

"Touch one."

He laughed. "Because me checking out another dude's tats in the middle of campus isn't weird enough?"

"Just do it." I slumped so he could better reach them.

The palm of his hand ran over the length of one of the feathers. "There's something rough under it. Scar?"

Acidic bile stung the back of my throat. I'd never told anyone why I'd gotten the tattoos on my eighteenth birthday. The only person at college who knew was Junkyard, and only because he'd known me before I'd gotten them.

I closed my eyes and swallowed. "I have no memories of my father holding me, playing with me, or feeding me. None. I was three when he went to prison, so why would I? But I can still hear the son of a bitch laughing when he held the hot cigarette lighter to my back. I can still feel his weight on top of me, pinning me while I screamed and thrashed. He did it seven times, and I have exactly seven memories of him."

Luther pulled his hand away and I slid my shirt back on.

"I'm sorry, man."

"No." I grabbed his shoulders. "We're done with being sorry. We're done with letting these fuckers run our lives. Promise me you'll give it your all. For us, not them."

"I will."

We entered the stadium through a field level entrance. Several people were gathered in the middle, grassy area of the track. I scanned the bleachers as we walked to join them. I didn't see Neyle—or anyone really.

I'd lingered after our most recent counseling session to confirm with Neyle he would get Luther's father to campus. Neyle said he was working on it.

"Where's the camera?" Luther asked.

"I'm sure they're up in the press box where they film all of the track meets." I lied but hoped Neyle was actually there.

Big stood amidst a small group of people wearing black shorts—only a touch longer than Luther's—and gray, "Army" shirts. Abbey, Sing, and Baker were off to one side chatting. They looked like lighthouses in their vibrant workout clothes compared to the ROTC crew. Luther joined them as I walked over to Big.

"Nice touch." I nodded to his group. "You ready?"

His eyes bulged with an evil grin. "Are you?"

"I guess—"

"Then fall in, Demps," Big bellowed. "That goes for everyone. Fall in."

I jogged into a formation line with the others, trying to shake Big's voice from my ringing from my ears. Big stood in front of us, his arms coiled around his chest like two bulging pythons. I scanned the actual military participants in the line and tried to mimic their posture and spacing.

"3rd Reserve Officers' Training Corps Brigade cadets

and … friends. Count off and stay in formation, or you'll get my special kind of *attention*. And I ain't your valentine or your mama. Cadets, is my special kind of attention something you want?"

"No, sir!"

"Thought not. I'm 'bout to make y'all Army strong. Jumping jacks, sound off. One, two—"

Five minutes into the jumping jacks, my legs were burning so badly I no longer cared if Luther's parents were watching. This was about surviving Big now. If we slowed, he screamed. If we went too fast, he screamed. He had us drop into push-up position next.

"Luther, front and center," Big shouted.

Luther took a tentative step forward.

"I've got time for a lot of things, but you ain't one of 'em. Move."

Luther sprinted next to him.

"Lead us, sir." Big smacked Luther on the back so hard he stumbled forward.

Luther's chin angled up and his eyes narrowed. He looked ready to close the game."Drop and give me thirty. Keep those butts down or I don't count them."

Big laughed, falling in beside me. "Kid's a natural."

I counted out my first two push-ups. "Well … *three* … he's had a lot of practice bossing people around in video games … *four*."

We went right into sit-ups afterward. Luther did them with us—him facing us, us facing him. Luther did two for every one he counted off, and halfway through our set of fifty he stood. Still counting, he walked between our lines like a seasoned drill instructor, encouraging and prodding when needed.

Next, Big marched us to the track us in two parallel lines.

"We go two miles. If you run, walk, get dragged by your hair, or propelled by my boot on your ass across that finish line, it makes no difference to me. But you *will* finish. Hop to it."

Baker, who jogged along next to me, winked. "Will you carry me if I fall, bro?"

"No." I laughed, still a little breathless from the sit-ups. "But I'll send Big back for you. No man left behind, Baker."

I thought I noticed an uptick in his pace after that. We'd finished our third lap when someone cried out behind me. Before I could react, Luther bolted by.

"Keep moving," Big shouted from the front.

I spun around, backpedaling to keep my pace. Several yards behind us, Sing was down on the turf, holding her ankle. Luther was at her side. I took off. I'd covered half the distance between us when Luther spotted me.

He waved frantically. "I'll help her. Keep going."

I glanced up at the press box. This was crap, she needed help, and Luther needed to show his dad he could hang with the ROTC guys. "You've got to finish."

"I'll catch up. Go," he said.

He'd already gotten her to her feet, so I obeyed. By the time I'd completed my next lap, Sing was lying on one of the benches surrounding the track, her foot elevated by Luther's wadded up T-shirt.

I reached the end of my eighth and final lap ahead of Abbey and Baker, but behind the ROTC crew. Those guys were professional runners in my book, and probably afraid of what Big would do to them if they let me win.

Soon, Abbey trotted to a stop next to me, panting. "Shouldn't we finish?"

"I want to wait on Luther." I held my hand over my eyes to search for him. He and Baker were halfway around the track.

With help from one of the ROTC members, Sing hobbled next to us. Baker stopped every few feet as he and Luther covered the last thirty yards. Each time, he'd put his hands on his knees and cough violently. And each time, Luther jogged in place beside him clapping his hands until Baker got going again.

Big led the ROTC group in cheering them on and we joined in. Baker stumbled across the finish and fell onto his back, wheezing.

"Are you done?" Luther stopped in front of us. His chest heaved, showing the outline of his ribs with every breath.

"We wanted to cross with you," I said.

Luther shook his head. "No. I'm not crossing until I've made sure everyone on my team has made it."

I smiled, no longer caring what his dad's reaction was going to be. Abbey and I helped Sing across. When Luther followed, we surrounded him.

I rubbed his head and hugged him. "You made it."

He looked up at me, his dark skin gleaming with pearls of sweat. "*We* made it."

Big shook his hand. "That was as fine a display of leadership as I've seen. I gotta tell you, when Ernie asked me to do this, I thought he'd lost his mind. Well, lost even more of his mind. But I'm glad I witnessed that."

"Excuse me … excuse me. I need to have a talk with my son."

The voice was unfamiliar, deep, and commanding. Luther's eyes went wide with the sound. The hairs on my neck stood from the pure terror in his expression. It had to be his father.

We parted to let the man through. His features could have been carved with a razorblade, all deep lines and sharp angles. He was lean and bespectacled, making the resemblance to Luther all that much more pronounced.

"Dad, what are you—"

"It seems I was led here on false pretenses. Your mother said I needed to meet with someone about your grades. Instead, I witnessed this silly display."

"Now wait a second." I tried to step to Luther's side, but he pushed me back.

"Dad, I've got something to say to you."

His father's lip curled. "I'll talk. You'll listen."

"You listen." Luther's chest swelled, as did mine. "You don't get to talk to me like that anymore. I'm not a child, and I'm not one of your soldiers."

"Oh, you're right about that. Soldiers aren't made by running a few laps with their buddies."

Big stepped in front of Luther's father completely obscuring his body from my line of sight. "Sir, with all due respect, I think your son would make a fine officer."

"And who are you?"

The veins on Big's neck throbbed. "I'm one of the future leaders of your Army, sir." Big motioned to his fellow cadets. "We all are. And we'd be proud to have someone like Luther among us. Come on cadets."

One by one, the ROTC members shook Luther's hand and left until it was only Abbey, Baker, Sing, Luther, and me standing in front of his dad.

Luther stepped up to his father. "I'm not afraid of you anymore. Take away my lunch money. Call me names—whatever you want. But I'm done."

His dad raised his hand, and I thought he would hit Luther. I tensed, preparing to jump between them. I would have gone to jail or gotten killed, but he wasn't going to lay a hand on my friend so long as I was breathing.

He lowered his fist. "You don't know what you're saying. What's gotten into you?"

Luther turned to us. "Them. Now go home and don't come back until you're ready to treat me like a man. Because a man is all you're going to find the next time you come looking."

His father spun on his heels and left, so he didn't see the tears drifting down Luther's face. I was very thankful for Luther's sake, but God, did I wish that fucker would have had to share that painful sight with me.

Chapter Twenty-Four

Luther strode over to me, his fists balled into pink and purple-tinged knots rage. I stiffened my jaw to brace for the blow. If I'd ever had anything coming in my life, it was this.

"Why didn't you tell me Dad was coming? I know you knew." He spun to face the others. "Did *you*?"

I maneuvered back into his line of fire. "No. This was all me. I'm sorry. So, so sorry. I thought—"

"What? That you could fix everything that's screwed up in my life in one morning? Guess what, Ernie? Things are definitely worse now."

I squeezed my eyes shut, wishing he would have hit me. It would have hurt less.

Her arm draped over Baker's shoulder for support, Sing moved between us. "That's not fair. He was only trying to help."

Luther turned away from us. "You don't get it—none of you do. We have chronic diseases. There's no cure for us.

We treat symptoms to make us feel like we're okay when we're not. We're never fucking okay."

He walked away. We didn't follow. Neyle emerged from one of the darkened tunnels that led onto the field. Luther blew right by him. I collapsed onto the track.

What had I done? I'd been so caught up with Margery and my own stuff that I hadn't seen my actions with the group for what they were. Luther was right. We were sick, and I'd been playing doctor like a little kid plays house.

Neyle hobbled up. "You need to get that looked at," he said to Sing. "I called Laura. She's waiting in her car in the parking lot. Can the two of you get her out there okay?"

Abbey nodded, sliding under Sing's other arm.

I stayed on the ground, head in my hands. *We are never okay.* Luther's words looped over and over in my thoughts, making me dizzy and nauseous.

After a long while, Neyle spoke. "I tried to beat him down, but the elevators are slow." He chuckled humorlessly.

"Why didn't you stop me?" The words were hoarse and dry coming out of my mouth, like trying to spit dust.

Neyle adjusted his weight to his cane. "Because growing is painful, both to do and to see."

"What does that even mean?"

"You've all grown from this trial. You couldn't know it, but Laura has known for weeks. The others told her in their individual sessions. After we talked the other night, I went to her dead-set on putting an end to this. Do you know what she told me?" He tapped my foot with his cane. "That I needed to trust you — them. That I needed to let you all grow."

"This feels more like dying."

"Ernie, I knew this wouldn't end well with Luther's father. He's a bully and makes statues appear flexible by comparison. He's done growing, and he's never going to change. But do you know what?"

I shook my head.

"Today, Luther accepted that truth. He is resolved to continue his life with or without his father's approval. There's only one way to deal with a bully. Stand up to him. I've tried for two semesters to get him to that point, and you accomplished it in a few weeks."

"Guess that makes me a saint." I pushed to my feet. "Or at least a damn good martyr."

"No. But it does make you a damn good friend." Neyle patted my shoulder. "Don't be too hard on yourself. Luther is going to be fine. So will you."

I wasn't so sure. I needed validation of my ability to bring others happiness instead of grief. I needed Margery. So I went to her.

A pickup truck with a South State bumper sticker was parked in front of her house when I arrived. I yanked my motorcycle helmet off and wiped the sweat from my brow with the back of my arm. The sick feeling I'd had since Luther's blowout intensified, and then turned into something altogether poisonous. *Anger.*

Had Margery already moved on? Was I just her guy on the side? That didn't seem to fit her, but this thing between us had happened so quickly, I might have missed something critical…

I extended my hand to bang on her door, and then pulled it back. *Calm down. You should have called first.* Raised voices came from inside. *Trust your instincts. Get the hell out of here.* I took a cautious step backward. The door flung open.

The Walrus glowered at me from the opening. We stared at each other for a long moment. I had no words, because all the air had vacated my lungs. Like a hiker stumbling upon an angry bear, I was glued to the ground, too shocked and scared to move.

"You son of a bitch." He lunged at me but was yanked back by Margery.

She ducked around him and put her finger in his chest. "Dad, stay out of this."

"I've stayed out of it long enough. That boy is poison. He's going to sink your career just like he sunk my goddamned team."

My face burned as rage and shame swept over me in equal proportion. He wasn't entirely wrong about me being poison. But even I didn't deserve to be talked to like that. Eventually, being pissed won out.

I stepped back onto the porch. "She's a grown woman. She can date whoever she damn well pleases. She isn't one of your players you can intimidate and order around."

Margery placed her other hand on my chest, separating us with her arms spread wide like a suspension bridge. "Ernie, I really don't need—"

"That's where you're wrong, hotshot." The Walrus sneered, a look of bloody victory smeared on his face. "She isn't free to date who she wants. She's a teacher. If word got out, she could be expelled from her graduate program. And the only way word doesn't get out is if she puts an end to this. Right now."

I balled my fists and would have taken a swing if not for Margery being in the way.

Her eyes bulged, and she jerked her attention back to her father. "Listen to yourself. You're threatening to sabotage your own daughter's career over a ridiculous vendetta with a student. What is wrong with you?"

His face reddened. "You don't know him. I'm trying to protect—"

Margery stomped her foot so hard, the sound made me flinch. "Shut up, go inside, or I'm never going to speak to you again."

The Walrus crossed his arms. His mouth opened to speak.

"Now," Margery said, her voice barely an audible growl.

After he'd gone back inside, she hooked my arm and dragged me from the porch. We reached the street and faced each other. Tears spilled from her eyes. My already scarred heart ripped in two with the sight of the anguish on her face. I reached out, intending to brush the tears away. My hand shook so badly, I thought I might put her eye out, so I grabbed a fistful of my own hair instead.

"How did he find out?" I knew the answer, but hearing David's name said out loud seemed like a necessary step before hunting him down and beating him to death.

Margery threw her hands up. "Does it matter, Ernie? He knows. End of story."

"Would he really turn you in?" Another question I probably knew the answer to.

She stared up at me, her lips trembling. No words were spoken, but her pained expression said plenty. A dagger of anger stabbed me. I'd given Luther a speech earlier about not being controlled by fathers anymore, and here was another one trying to screw my life over.

I kicked a rock across the road. "When you said end of story, did you mean the end of *our* story?"

She sobbed. "What choice do we have? He said he'd make sure you never played baseball here again—"

"I don't care about the team." I grabbed her arms. "I care about you."

Her head lowered. "That's just it. I care about you, too."

I tilted her chin up with my finger. I had to make her see beyond this somehow.

"Forget him, then. We tell him it's off and wait until the semester is over. Then he can do what he wants."

"You don't get it." She shook her head, flinging fresh tears from her cheeks. "He'll make phone calls. He said the pro teams would know about what you did. You might never play baseball again. I can't take that from you."

My insides felt like they'd been scooped out. If not for the sound of my pulse in my ears, I might have actually believed it.

"I'm sorry, Ernie. I don't know what else to do."

She was right. He could make our lives a living hell if he wanted. I walked to my bike.

"Are you okay?" She reached out to me, her fingers clawing the air as if she could pull me back to her. "Where are you going?"

I stared at her, trying to lock the image of her beckoning me into my mind. Who knew if I'd ever get to see it again?

"To pay it forward." I revved the motorcycle's engine to an earsplitting roar and sped off.

Chapter Twenty-Five

I stopped at a random parking lot to dial Junk.

"Yo."

"What are you up to tonight?"

I used the speakerphone so I didn't have to remove my helmet. There was a slight delay. My words echoed back to me, adding to the feeling that I was in the middle of a waking nightmare.

"Nada. What's up?"

"Let's go out."

Junkyard whooped. "I'll get my dancing shoes and some rubbers. The Hawk and the Dog are going on the prowl."

I tapped the phone off. A stillness came over me. I drifted into the eye of an emotional hurricane. When I came out the other side, the storm would rage.

A few minutes later, I knocked on Junk's door. He yanked it open and continued smacking his cheeks with Old Spice. "Why are your eyes so red?"

"Allergies."

Junk nodded. "Always a bitch this time of year. Figured you staying off the field would help, though."

I shrugged.

He grinned. "I called around. Darko's got a party in the works. Think Dead Eye wants to tag along?"

I squinted, straining to block out the piercing headache I'd developed and process his question. "Who?"

"The skinny kid with the glasses you've been hanging out with. He's an alright little dude."

If I'd had another ounce of emotion left, thinking of Luther might have wrung it out of me. But I'd already bled out. My give-a-shit was gone.

"I don't think Luther would want to come tonight."

"Then let's ride."

Darko's was as packed as I'd ever seen it. The parties near the end of the semester were always the best that way. Everyone wanted to say good-bye, figure out who'd be on campus over the summer, or try to get lucky one last time.

The lawn was littered with people and discarded bottles. Junk and I picked our way through the crowd. I let him do all the talking. Trying to find words was like trying to swallow a spoonful of sand—an exercise in discomfort and bitterness. So I didn't bother.

"I need alcohol," I said to him after we'd said our fifth hello.

His eyes locked onto mine. "You going to tell me what's up?"

I shook my head.

"Alcohol it is."

I couldn't tell Junk I was planning on beating David senseless if I found him, because he'd clearly try to stop me. He returned with three beers. I took two of them.

"Will you make sure I get back to the dorms?"

"The fuck kind of question is that? You know I will."

"If you see any of the other guys from the team, come find me." I pulled my baseball hat down and faded into the crowd.

It was the strangest feeling, wanting to be left alone but knowing that fulfilling that desire would be fatal. Shoulders collided with mine as I slithered from room to room trying to find a good rock to crawl under. I found my spot in the television room. There was a dirty recliner wedged into a far corner to make way for mingling. Not a boulder, but it'd do.

I plucked two more beers from a cooler, gave the guy guarding it a couple of bucks, and drifted back to the chair. People wandered in and out of the room, but it was generally kind of smelly and dark, so no one stayed long. The lone exception was a long couch along one wall that seemed to be a make out magnet. The thought of touching another girl quickly turned to poison in my mind, so I tried to focus on my drinks when the couples there got a little too rambunctious.

"I said I'm not interested."

The familiar female tone of the voice brought me out of my grim fog.

"Abbey?" I scooted to the edge of my chair.

She stood inside of the doorway that led to the kitchen. A guy's arms were on either side of her, pinning her between them.

"C'mon. Could be fun."

That familiar male voice brought a new kind of haze over me. A red one. My fingers tightened around the bottle in my hand. While I'd fantasized about finding David here, I honestly hadn't thought my luck would be this great.

"Nope. Still not interested. I need to find my friends —"

"We could go over to that couch for a few minutes. You'll forget all about your friends when I'm done."

An electric current of hate swept over me as I moved behind them. My fists tingled with anticipation. He had already destroyed my relationship with Margery. Now, he was coming onto one of my best friends who definitely wasn't interested. He might as well have typed up a motivational guide for wanting to kick his ass and e-mailed it to me.

David grabbed her arm as I grabbed his.

"What the fu —"

I flung him backward into the TV room. He collided with a bookcase loaded with bottles, sending them crashing to the floor. People fled from the room, but more ran in.

"Fight," someone shouted, but the sound of my thundering pulse almost blotted it out.

David's eyes blazed when he realized who'd interfered.

"Get up." My breath whistled between my clinched teeth as I spoke. I pitched my hat off to the side.

He scrambled to his feet. "Your girlfriend told you the bad news, huh?"

I launched into David, crashing us into a wall. The paneling caved behind our weight. He caught me in the chest with an elbow, sending me stumbling away. While he tried to stand, I moved back in. I punched him in the nose and felt his bones crunching underneath my knuckles. He fell back on his ass.

Arms wrapped around me from behind before I could get on top of him. "Stop it."

"Let me go." I managed to twist and shove the person off.

Bash glared at me, his stupid flat bill hat knocked askew from the struggle.

"Stay out of this, Bash. This is between David and me."

"No, it's not." He pounded his chest with his hand. "It's me you've got a beef with."

I raised my fists. "What are you talking about?"

His head drew back. "I'm the one who told coach.

All of the tension in my body uncoiled at once, and I stumbled backward. "Why? I thought we were friends?"

"Yeah, I thought the same thing. But I was wrong." He shook his head. "All you've ever cared about is yourself, and how the world has shit all over you. Well guess what? That doesn't give you the right to smear it on the rest of us."

"You don't realize what you've done." Feeling returned to my numbed legs as anger took hold of me once again. I stepped toward him, pointing. "If you had a problem, you should have come to me first."

He spread his arms out wide. "If you want to take a shot, do it. But I'm not sorry. You screwed us over. You screwed *me* over. We're not friends, Ernie. People like you don't have any."

My shoulders dropped more with each of his words until my fury had all but sloughed away. He was right. I'd used Luther and the group to make me feel better about myself. Junk had been my sturdy emotional crutch for so long, I had no idea what he was. Margery might not be anything more than my lust playing out.

A blow from behind sent me flying forward. I collided with Bash, forcing us both to the ground in a heap. *David.*

He dragged me to my feet and punched me in the gut before I could get my bearings. My vision blurred with tears as I sucked at air that wouldn't come.

"What's going on here?" Junkyard bellowed.

David socked me in the jaw as I turned toward the sound. I stumbled into a bookshelf and grabbed a beer bottle. I let David pull me back by my shirt, and then broke the bottle over the side of his head. Blood covered his ear as he careened sideways cursing me.

I was going to choke the last breath from his body with my bare hands —

Someone yanked my shirt. "Ernie, no."

I spun with my fist balled. Abbey put her hands up to shield her face.

"Cops," someone shouted

The word cut through my rage and I looked at Abbey. "Are you okay?"

Her jaw trembled. "I'm fine — look out!"

David barreled into me. The impact thrust me into Abbey, sending her flying. I punched, gouged, and scratched as David and I wrestled for position. I finally got him in a headlock.

People ran in every direction. Bash sprinted from the room. Junk helped Abbey to her feet.

"Get her out of here." I adjusted my grip each time David would thrash.

"What about you?" Junk asked, adrenaline making him wild-eyed and jumpy.

"Go."

"Don't kill him," Junk said, dragging Abbey from the room.

I tightened my hold. David gurgled...

"Let him go." The cop had a Taser in his hand. He yelled something into a walkie-talkie clipped to his shoulder. Two more officers flanked him within seconds.

I let my body go limp. David slid to the floor, choking. Rough hands seized my arms, yanking me to my feet. The handcuffs clamped over my wrists. The cold metal against my skin brought me back to hard reality. I'd crashed. Now the burning would begin.

By virtue of trying to kill David, I got my own cell. Wisely, the police thought it a bad idea to slap us in the same drunk tank together, so I was shuffled off to my own tiny plot of taxpayer-provided seclusion. I stretched out on the metal cot, wincing each time my jaw throbbed, and contemplating all of the idiotic choices I'd made.

Deciding to get kicked off the baseball team instead of simply quitting. *Check.* Getting into a relationship—with the coach's daughter no less—when I couldn't even take care of myself. *Check.* Interfering in my friend's lives until they hated me. *Check.* Drinking and fighting to fix the problems in my life. *Check.*

I groaned thinking about the last one. As if my life wasn't going up in flames fast enough, I felt compelled to fling a little gasoline on the pyre. At least I was thorough when it came to self-implosion. And I'd accomplished my goal. I was as alone as I'd ever been in my life. There was no one left to hurt, so I kicked the cinderblock wall the bed butted against.

The metal look-through on the door slid open. I jumped with the sound. I'd dozed off.

An officer's face filled the opening. "You've got a visitor. Stay away from the door."

Had my ex-girlfriend of a few hours, or the friends I'd completely let down, bail me out? Hard to imagine, but my pulse quickened with hope nonetheless.

The Walrus entered. My chest deflated with a sigh. I doubted he was here to throw me a lifeline. There were heavy bags under his eyes, and his cheeks were flushed to a familiar shade of crimson. He'd been screaming at someone. Probably lots of someones. Half the team had been at that party, and who knew how many of them had been hauled in.

He sat on the toilet, and I couldn't help but find a little humor in that. His hands combed through his hair too many times to count before he finally spoke. "Explain yourself."

I laughed. Of all the people in the world I currently owed an explanation to, he wasn't one of them. Wasn't as if he couldn't put the pieces together, and I'd be damned if I'd give him the satisfaction of getting me to revisit his victory at Margery's. He'd split us up and finally gotten his revenge on me for all of the grief I'd brought into his life. He could only be here to gloat.

I situated myself on the bed so my back rested against the wall.

"That's right, smart guy. Keep thinking this is a game. I'll let you in on a little secret. You're in a big shit pond with no waders on this time, my friend. If David presses charges, you could get booked on aggravated assault. That's a felony last I checked. Not only would you be facing a couple months behind bars and your college days be over, but any chance you had at a playing pro ball would be a fart in the wind, too. Still having fun?"

My mouth went dry. He had a point. Anything before this would've been his word against mine. But a felony would be a deal breaker for most teams, no questions asked.

I moved to the edge of the cot. "Why'd you come here?"

He smiled an ugly, sneering scowl of a grin. "Because I've finally got you by the shorthairs, boy. You've done nothing but make a mockery of all I've worked for and achieved professionally since you set foot on campus. I regret the day Coach Ramirez first sat you down in front of me, and if he weren't such a goddamned good recruiter, I'd fire his ass for it."

"Leave me alone, then. You've got what you wanted. I'm screwed. The match goes to you."

He shook his head. "If I only could. In one final kick of sand in my face, the Universe decided to let you meet my daughter. She's more stubborn than you'll ever know, and smarter still. My ultimatum to not see you again will last until the semester ends. I had no leverage to make her give you up. Until now."

Hearing her name again churned my already agitated guts. I let my head thud against the wall behind me.

"What's your deal?" I closed my eyes to brace for the impact.

"I'll talk to David and get him to not press charges. The cops will want him to, of course. But I've got some pull in this town. I think I can convince them some of my boys had a little too much to drink and let their roughhousing get out of hand. I'll even get you out of here."

"And I have to do what in exchange?"

"You swear to me you'll never come back to this school when the semester is over. You'll never talk to Margie again. Ever. Coach Ramirez told me he's gotten some offers for you. Pick out whatever team you want to go play for and enjoy your next life. That's the bargain."

I eyed him, not feeling the need to explain I'd already reached most of those terms on my own. My fight was over. I'd successfully destroyed every last good thing for me at this school. Mom's promise was already a scorched silhouette on the wall of my psyche.

I closed my eyes, not wishing to be someplace else, simply wishing to not be. "Okay."

Chapter Twenty-Six

The sun was barely cresting the horizon when I'd walked onto the English building's rooftop. Campus was dead this early on a Saturday, but I figured the custodians would have the buildings open for cleaning. I'd tried a couple of doors and eventually found one unlocked. Then it was a simple matter of taking the stairwell to the top. Someone had wedged a rock in the door—probably so they could sneak onto the roof to smoke and not get locked out.

Feeling like I'd been pushed to the edge had left me wondering what it actually looked like. So I'd come to the tallest building on campus to find out.

I hopped up on the ledge and dangled my feet over. I closed my eyes and let the stiff breeze rock me with each gust. The birds came more alive with each golden finger of sunlight that stretched over the grounds below, as more of me shut down. I'd been such a damned fool to think my life was evolving. The sun dangled in front of me as one big ball of brightly hued, gassy proof. I was revolving right along with the earth under my feet. Nothing would really change, just come full-circle again. My seasons were locked in stone, and with every brilliant summer, there'd be an equally bleak winter to follow.

I'm never getting out of this cycle.

I leaned out over the edge and spat. The wind scuttled the wad away before it reached halfway to the ground. I wondered if the draft might lift me up as well.

"Say 'dare, honey. You want to be careful now."

I swung my legs around back to the roof side and spied the groundskeeper resting against a large air duct. The smoke from his pipe mingled with steam coming from the vents and created intermittent smog around him. From where I sat, he could have easily been mistaken for an old, hunched gray gargoyle lazing in the early morning shadows.

How long had he been there?

He shuffled in my direction. I rose to meet him, but he waved his hands for me to sit.

"Ol' Willy didn't wanna fuss. I meant to leave you be but reckoned you might be thinking about making a mess I didn't want to clean."

He cackled, ripping a smile from my lips. It was as if Willy had lit a candle in the dark cavern of my thoughts. Still, grinning made my face hurt, so I resumed what I imagined to be a pouty scowl.

"What are you doing up here, Willy?"

He tapped the pipe on the heel of his boot to empty the ashes, never taking his large, bloodshot eyes off of me. "Oh, same as you I 'spect. Tending the ol' noggin garden a bit." He pointed to his head. "Them weeds crop up thick 'n fierce if you don't thin 'em out every now and then. Expect I'm hiding, too. These days, a lot of folk don't approve of Willy's pipe. No sir."

He laughed again, and I joined him this time.

"No, I bet not."

"Watch you doing up here, anyhow?"

I shrugged. "Thinking."

His eyes narrowed. "Bout what?"

The curve of his arched brow made me feel I could read his thoughts like they were written out in the wrinkles of his brown skin. My first instinct was to reassure him that I wasn't *really* considering the big plunge. But that seemed disingenuous somehow.

"Life ... I guess."

"So long as you still thinking 'bout livin' it, no harm dare."

I squinted at the sky before returning my gaze to him. "Willy, have you ever screwed things up?"

"Well, sure I have."

I sighed. "No, I mean have you ever screwed *all* the things up?"

He pawed at the silver stubble on his chin. "Dare was dis one time, not long after I first started here. Fact is, I thought I had hold of the fertilizer when it was really killer. I done a number on the beds that day for sure, honey. And old Willy's boss was mad-to-fight-a-bear for sure."

"What did you do?"

More cackles. "Well, first I called my late wife an' told her to put the beans back on, 'cause Willy had jus' stepped in it to his knees. She weren't none too happy. We just had a new one, and we were fierce poor, understand. You know what that woman told me?"

I shook my head.

"*Willy*, she says, *you go tell dat man you'll grow him twice as many new ones.* I told her, 'Woman, I done said, I killed 'em all, ain't no way I can make 'em come back.' *No*, she says, *Ain't nothing killed for good unless you just quit tending to it. So go on an git to tending.*"

"Did it work?"

"Took me two years, but sure did. Fact, that's how the President's garden started. Thought Willy did such a good job, they wanted mo'."

"Sounds like your wife was a smart lady."

"No, honey, but she were meaner than an ol' one-eyed dog on a bone. That's for sure."

He slapped his knee and wheezed out more laughter.

"Ernie," a familiar male voice shouted up to me.

I'd forgotten I'd had my back to the ledge. I peeked over to the ground below.

Luther waved his arms frantically. "Don't— "

The wind gusted and ate up his voice.

"What?" I leaned farther out to try to hear him.

"Don't jump, please!" He had a cell phone in his hand.

Oh shit. They think I'm about to call it a life.

I held up my hands. "Hey, it's—"

221

A campus security golf cart skidded to a stop next to him. Neyle and Abbey hopped off the back.

Oh double shit.

Neyle pointed up with his cane. "Ernie, you stay right there. Everything's going to be okay."

I waved, trying to smile wide enough they'd see that I was okay and in relatively good spirits. Neyle said something to the security guard using wild gestures. Maybe smiling while sitting on a ledge hadn't been the best idea...

I turned to Willy. "I better take care of this."

We'd made it halfway across the roof when the steel door banged open. Margery stumbled through. "Ernie, where are—"

Our eyes locked. I held my arms high above my head to absorb the collision as she slammed into me with a hug. I was still freshly bruised from the fight with David, so her hold on me was painful. But I'd never experienced discomfort that welcome in my life.

"You shit. We were scared to death." Her words were muffled against my chest.

I kissed the top of her head. "I'm okay. Really."

Willy touched his forehead in a mock-salute and I nodded. I waited until he'd exited before pushing Margery to arm's length. "How did you find me here?"

She slapped my stomach. "You're an asshole. Abbey called Neyle when you got arrested. After a million phone calls, he figured out you'd been released. We spent half the night looking ... you're still an asshole."

I smiled and pulled her back into a hug. "I shouldn't

have—"

"Shush." She glared at me, tears skidding down her face. "I should've stood up to Dad in the first place. I'm going to resign from teaching the class on Monday."

"I can't let you do that."

"You're not *letting* me do anything. This isn't only your fault, Ernie. You don't hold the fate of the world in your hands, damn it."

"I know." I dipped my head to kiss her.

The door banged open again. Abbey ran through, followed by Luther, Baker, Junk, and Sing. They'd come for me. All of them. I swallowed back a lump in my throat.

Abbey ran to us, her arms outstretched. "Thank God you're okay. I wanted to talk to you at the station, but the cops wouldn't let me out of questioning."

"Why were you there?" I put a shaky hand on her shoulder. "Did you get into trouble because of me—"

She squeezed my arm. "Not at all. And neither are you."

I cursed under my breath. "I know. I had to make a deal with Coach."

"What kind of deal?" Margery's hold on me tightened.

There was more than a trace of warning in her voice. I lowered my head. I didn't want to tell her now. Or ever, really. Especially if that meant she'd let go of me again.

Abbey laughed, bringing my attention back to her. "Ernie, everything is fine. I told the cops that you thought David was trying to assault me and you stopped it. They're not charging you with anything. David, on the other hand, is getting a drunk and disorderly."

I had no words to tell Abbey how happy she'd made me, so I hugged her instead. I swung her around in a full circle. The others crowded around us. Most of them looked bewildered or concerned.

Sing smiled. "You look like hell."

Margery returned to my side. I rubbed my neck trying to massage a response from my brain that justified all the trouble I'd caused them. I had nothing.

"I ... I needed some air."

Luther smirked. "There are places closer to the ground, you know."

Junkyard punched me gently on the shoulder. "I can't take you anywhere."

"Sorry, buddy. In fact..." I made eye contact with each of them. "I apologize to all of you. I never understood that by trying to help you, I was really working through my own problems. It was selfish and dumb. I've believed for a long time that being alone would fix things for me. What I really needed, was friends who believed in who I was, not just in what I could do. I needed you all."

"We helped you?" Luther asked.

I nodded, blinking away stinging tears. "Very much so."

"Then we're even." He wrapped his arms around Margery and me.

Junk hugged all three of us tight enough to make me squirm. Soon, Baker, Abbey, and Sing added to the group embrace. We stayed joined together on the roof a long time, each of us uncertain pioneers in our own lives, witnesses to the dawning of an unexpected new day.

Chapter Twenty-Seven

Finals brought an unceremonious end to our merry band. Luther and I grabbed lunch together a couple of times. He planned to stick around campus over the summer and take a class or two. He'd also enrolled in a computer-programming course at the local tech school, figuring it was a way he could pursue his computer interests and not completely abandon what he'd started in college. His mother had slipped him the money to pay for it.

I saw Baker at the bookstore once. He'd be "rocking out by a pool and jamming with friends" all summer.

Junk was heavy into getting ready for summer baseball. He'd made a traveling college all-star team based out of Wisconsin, so his break would be spent exploring shithole towns, raising hell, and banging the locals—his words. We'd stay in touch.

Sing had already finished classes and headed back to Taiwan to visit her parents. But in a sign of true growth, she'd added all of us to her online friends lists. Even Baker. She'd said, "It's perfect. I don't have to smell him this way."

I went to the Fredrick House to say good-bye to Neyle and Laura. But instead of going inside, I sat on the porch, flicking through poetry on my phone. Maybe I was stalling for time because I didn't know how to properly bid farewell. And maybe I needed to read some opening lines from Lord Byron's *The Corsair* to get some perspective on where I'd come to.

Our thoughts are boundless, and our souls are free –
These are our realms, no limits in their sway

Whatever I did next would always be up to me. The sound of the bell on the counseling center door jingling made me jump. Abbey walked out carrying a stack of flyers.

"Out to spread more of Neyle's propaganda?" I grinned.

"Ernie, I thought you'd already left for the semester."

I stood to greet her with a hug. "They haven't gotten rid of me yet."

"Got any big plans for the summer?" she asked.

I shrugged. "I've got a few intriguing possibilities. What about you?"

"Taking two classes and working here."

"Really? That's great."

She smiled. "Yep. The student secretary is graduating, and Laura asked if I wanted the job. I think I might actually look into becoming a counselor someday. I'll have to change my major, again, of course."

"I think you'd be brilliant, Abbey. Both as a counselor and the student secretary. The last girl was a little grumpy."

She held up the flyers. "I'm putting these up around campus. We're promoting an eating disorder seminar Dr. Laura is putting on. I'm going to speak at it."

"Nervous?"

Her eyes bulged. "I'm totally freaking out. What about you? Am I going to see you again next semester?"

"Still not sure. I'm done playing baseball here, though."

She squeezed my arm. "It'll work out, Ernie."

So long as I have good friends, I could have added.

"I really think so, too."

She waved goodbye and said, "You know where to find me next fall. Don't be a stranger."

Neyle wasn't in the basement, so I wandered upstairs. There wasn't anyone at the front desk, either, but voices came from Laura's office.

The door was cracked, so I gave a soft knock. "Can I come in?"

Laura beamed when I poked my head in. "We'd be upset if you didn't."

Neyle lazed on the old leather couch, his cane placed in his lap. He adjusted to make room for me. "The Prodigal Son returns."

I smiled. "Well, he *did* have an appointment."

Laura pushed her chair over to be able to sit in front of us. She had a folder in her hand. After slipping on her reading glasses, she glanced over the pages.

"I don't think we need this." She dropped the folder unceremoniously to the ground next to her. "Ernie, how do you think your semester went?"

"Well ... it was certainly *different.*"

"How so?"

I laughed. "Contrary to popular opinion, I hadn't planned on sabotaging my baseball career. And I definitely hadn't counted on meeting a girl, or making friends with my counseling group. Oh, and there was the night in jail."

"See, Laura?" Neyle chuckled. "This is why I never wanted to leave college. What an adventure."

"Sometimes I think you didn't leave." She gave him a disapproving look. "You feel like you benefited from the counseling experience?" she asked me.

I regarded each of them. They were calm, interested, and caring—or displaying what I'd come to know as the *counselor face*. The first thing that crossed my mind was to tell them how they'd changed my life. But that wasn't quite right.

"You saved my life."

Laura shook her head. "No, *you* saved your life. We simply believed you could do it."

"Wait a second," Neyle said. "I recall buying him some ice cream along the way. And don't forget the jellybeans." He laughed.

"Oh hush," Laura said in a sweet, scolding tone. "Tell us about your plans going forward. I understand you've run into some issues with your scholarship?"

"Yeah, I think my days pitching for South State are over. Coach hated me before I started dating his daughter against his wishes. I figured it was best not to put myself in his path everyday."

"Probably a wise move." She studied me. "Your relationship with her is going forward then?"

"That's what I'm about to find out."

Margery answered her door wearing a puffy, floral-patterned blouse, draped so it exposed one bare shoulder, and khaki shorts. She had a cup of tea in one hand and a record in the other.

My God, how I hope some things will never change.

"How'd you do on that English lit final?" she asked offhandedly as I followed her through the house.

"Not sure. The teacher is a real hard ass though."

She placed her tea and the album on a nearby table. "Well, you had better see what you can do to soften her up."

I pulled her body against mine and we kissed. "I still can't believe they let you finish out the semester." I brushed her hair away from her face with my thumbs.

She smiled. "When it came down to it, I wasn't *technically* considered a teacher. While not so good for the ego, it certainly helped my case. I'd done them a favor by pitching in so they didn't have to cancel the course mid-semester. In return, they did me a favor by not ruining my career before it got started."

"Seems a fair exchange."

"Uh-huh, and speaking of fair exchange, how about a little something for my trouble?"

She slid her hands underneath my shirt and ran her fingers along my ribs.

Her touch tickled me into squirming. "You, madam, are no lady."

"Exactly."

She shoved me backward onto the couch and straddled me. I kissed her but quickly pulled my head back.

"I've got something I need to talk to you about first."

She stared at me with a look of half frustration, half concern. "What about?"

"It's in my back pocket."

Her hands went searching and found the nest of papers I'd tucked away.

"More poetry?" A greedy smile pouted her lips.

"Not exactly."

"Damn."

She unfolded the papers, her lips moving silently as she poured over the first page.

"It's a contract..." Her gaze drifted up to meet mine. "To play baseball."

I nodded. "For the Kentucky Mudcats."

"How long?"

"Definitely over the summer. They can offer to re-up after that."

"What about school?"

"I don't know. But the pay is pretty good. So maybe I could afford it. I could probably take some classes closer to the team even—"

"What about us?"

"I was hoping you could help me with that one."

She dropped the contract and hopped off my lap. "I can't quit school and go with you if that's—"

"No." I grabbed her hands. "That's not what I'm after."

Her eyes widened. Was it terror or excitement I saw in them?

"Oh, God. Don't ask me *that*, Ernie. Not now—"

"No!" Had she thought I was going to ask her to marry me? My pulse soared, creating a dizzy, sickly feeling in my stomach. "Not *that* ... Margery, I have to play baseball. It's all I've got outside of us. It's all I've ever had. But I need you in my life, too. I need to know you'll stay with me if I pursue it. Will you?"

"Don't be silly. I'm not going anywhere, and, of course, I want you to play baseball."

That's not a yes.

"You'll stay with me as I figure out the next step?" My heart went from flying to a stop. Only one word would send it soaring again.

"Yes." She returned to my lap and kissed my cheek. "And maybe the next several after that."

Epilogue

The grass had been newly cut, but it didn't smell as crisp up here in the stands. Sitting on the hard, backless bleachers for two hours had left my legs numb and achy. Cold and damp, the conditions weren't ideal for baseball. Arms wouldn't be as loose, so the pitches would be slower, and the wet ground would make fielding an adventure. There was plenty of cheering, but none of it for me.

In spite of all that, this truly was a perfect moment, on a perfect day. My best friends and I had gathered to watch South State play for another shot at the championship series. I hoped this time would be different.

"Make him give you the high heat," I muttered to Junk as if he could hear me.

I crammed some more cotton candy in my mouth before Baker could eat it all.

The metal bat glinted as Junk waggled it, waiting on exactly the right pitch. He swung and missed.

"Damn it." I smacked my leg.

"He'll be okay," Margery said, but the way she perched on the edge of her seat and gnawed on her fingernails didn't do much to convince me.

Luther marked his scorecard and looked at me. The light reflecting off of his glasses hid his eyes, but I knew they'd be worried. The game could be won or lost on the next pitch.

"Full count," he said.

"You can do it," Abbey yelled from behind me. She had come to her feet, yanking Baker and Sing up with her.

"Yeah, don't suck," Sing shouted, then whacked me on the back of the head with her giant foam finger. "Stand up, loser."

Margery latched onto my arm, and we stood with the rest of the crowd. I took her hand in mine. Not having a baseball to fiddle with, I ran my fingers over the ridges of her ring in a repetitive, nervous pattern.

Luther started the chant. "Junk, Junk, Junk, Junk..."

Soon, we all joined in. The air in the stadium was electric, swelling and churning as the pitcher went through his pre-pitch routine. It felt like being in the middle of a human thundercloud.

Nearly a full year had passed since I'd been on a college baseball field in a similar position, but the nerves and expectations I'd felt were as fresh to me as the last memories of a great dream. I'd won a few pro games on last pitches already, but it didn't compare to this. I was here as a student, fan, and friend, making it feel as if the world would make its next revolution—or not—depending on the outcome of the next swing of the bat.

The ball flew from the pitcher's hand, and I had to look away. The *tink* of the bat making contact with the ball forced my gaze back to the field. People around me jumped up and down as it looped deep to left-center. The fielder had a good bead on it...

Margery and I hopped, too, screaming at the ball to fall.

The runner on third had already crossed home plate. Hands on his helmet, he could only wait for the ball to come down with the rest of us. Junk was halfway between first and second when the fielder lunged and missed. The ball skidded to the fence and the crowd erupted. We were going to the championship. At last.

A Note on Poetry

Several notable poems and poets were referenced throughout this story. All of which are found to be in the public domain. It was a real treat getting to spend time with these works under the guise of "research." If the words resonated with you, I'd encourage you to check out more from these folks:

(Listed in order of appearance.)
Robert Frost, *A Dream Pang* & *A Late Walk*
Lord Tennyson, *Ask Me No More*
Henry Vaughn, *The World*
William Wordsworth, *The Solitary Reaper*
Emily Dickinson, *Hope Is A Thing With Feathers*
Lord Byron, *The Corsair*

Acknowledgements

Writing this book was a journey, and I had many guides and companions along the way. Specifically, I'd like to thank:

My wife, Erin, who is beside me in all things. My family and friends, for all of their tireless love and encouragement. The vast writing community, for their inspiration and tutelage.

The early readers of this story, Morgan, Vicki, and Luanne. Your bravery in reading Ernest before an editor had gotten ahold of it/me speaks volumes of not only your friendship, but your pain tolerance. I have a tremendous amount of respect for all of you, and I hope I've successfully applied your wisdom.

My editors, Lynnette and Melissa. If there are any shiny bits in this story, I'm quite sure your polishing cloths have touched them.

My special friends Neyle and Laura, for gratuitous use of your names—and being patient with me. I told you I'd put you in a story!

Lastly, Dan Schafer for the use of the killer Methadones track in the book trailer. It gave me a ton of confidence when someone whose writing skills and creativity I admire so quickly embraced my vision for this project. Thanks for supporting your fellow creative types and encouraging what I'm trying to do to raise awareness for mental illness.

About the Author

Growing up in small-town Oklahoma, there were limits on the amount and types of entertainment at my disposal. Perhaps that's why I set my imagination free. After collecting degrees in psychology and counseling, life brought me to Missouri, Texas, and Northern California--where I currently read, write, and live. I fill my spare time playing video games, watching movies, planning for the zombie apocalypse, reading graphic novels, and playing with my dogs.

Website: www.ejwesley.com

Group Blog: www.naalley.com

Twitter: @EJWesley

Facebook: www.facebook.com/EJWesley

Goodreads: www.goodreads.com/EJWesley

Made in the USA
Lexington, KY
29 October 2014